STREET DUTY

Chris Ould has written more than eighty hours of television drama, including episodes of *Casualty* and over forty hours of the hugely-successful UK police drama *The Bill*, winning a BAFTA for one episode. Chris lives in Dorset with his wife and son. This is his debut YA novel.

STREET DUTY

case one: knock down

Chris Ould

For Rachel – at last, and without whom…

First published in the UK in 2012 by Usborne Publishing Ltd., Usborne House, 83-85 Saffron Hill, London EC1N 8RT, England. www.usborne.com

Cover photography: Hooded teenage girl © Justin Paget/Corbis, Background photography © George Logan/Corbis

A CIP catalogue record for this book is available from the British Library.

ISBN 9781409547280 JFMAMJJ SOND/12 00055/1

Printed in Reading, Berkshire, UK.

AUTHOR'S NOTE

The characters and events in this novel are fictitious. However, the law and police procedures – with the exception of the TPO training scheme – have been kept as close to reality as possible.

GLOSSARY

a body:	a person or officer
a brief:	a solicitor
CCTV:	closed-circuit television
CID:	Criminal Investigation Department
civvies:	civilians – members of the public. Also, civilian clothing
CPS:	Crown Prosecution Service
CSE:	Crime Scene Examiner
DC:	Detective Constable (plain clothes)
Delta Mike:	call sign for all officers and vehicles attached to Morningstar Road station
Delta Mike Five:	call sign for IRV
DI:	Detective Inspector
DS:	Detective Sergeant
FSS:	Forensic Science Services
IBO:	Integrated Borough Operations
IC1:	white person
IC3:	African/Afro-Caribbean person
index (number):	car registration number
intel:	intelligence information
IRV:	Instant Response Vehicle
ITU:	Intensive Therapy Unit
NFA:	No Further Action to be taken or required

OR:	Own Recognisance – independent working
PC:	Police Constable ("uniform")
PM:	paramedic
PR:	Personal Radio
refs:	refreshments – a meal break
reg:	a regular officer, i.e. a fully trained, full-time PC or above
RTC:	Road Traffic Collision
Section House:	residential accommodation for police officers
TPO:	Trainee Police Officer
turn:	a shift, e.g. early turn, late turn

POLICE RANKS
(IN ASCENDING ORDER)

Uniform

Trainee Police Officer

Police Constable

Sergeant

Inspector

Chief Inspector

CID

Detective Constable

Detective Sergeant

Detective Inspector

Detective Chief Inspector

HOME OFFICE PRESS RELEASE:

"The Trainee Police Officer programme is a pilot scheme which will enable the Police Service to enrol and train new recruits from the age of sixteen. Training will last two years, combining Academy study with Street Duty placement at selected operational stations.

On completion of the initial two-year training course, Trainee Police Officers will serve an additional year as Probationer PCs before joining their selected station as regular officers.

We anticipate that the TPO programme will enable the Police Service to more actively engage with younger elements of the community, as well as provide a fast-track entry to the Service for recruits demonstrating outstanding ability.

The TPO programme will be conducted on a trial basis in England and Wales and applicants will be chosen by selective interview. It is anticipated that the first intake of TPOs will number fifty, divided between three areas of the country: the South-west, North-east and the Midlands."

ENDS

FRIDAY

1

In the evening darkness it was hard to tell that Ashleigh Jarvis was crying as she hurried blindly across the uneven paving stones of the precinct. Her long dark hair straggled across her face and hid the tears. The racking sobs that welled up from her chest came silently, hard and choking.

But even if you couldn't tell that she was crying, you might have thought there was something odd about the way she moved. She hugged her arms tightly round her body, making her movements clumsy and off balance; but if you'd looked you'd probably have thought that it was just because she was cold. There was a chilly wind and her thin polyester cardigan clearly wasn't enough to retain any heat.

So, if you'd noticed Ashleigh Jarvis at all, you'd probably have seen just another silly fourteen year old who'd gone out without a coat – just trying to keep warm as she hurried to her destination. No one could really have known she was crying, or that she was hugging herself because it was the only way she knew to keep herself from collapsing in broken pieces on the ground.

No one did look at Ashleigh though – not closely; not with anything more than a passing glance. So no one stopped her to ask if she was okay. No one registered the fact that she was leaving bare footprints whenever she trod on dry flagstones after wet ones, and no one thought she wouldn't pause when she reached the kerb at the side of the road. In fact, no one really noticed her at all – not until they heard the skidding of tyres on tarmac and the surprisingly loud thud that came almost simultaneously.

No one saw the impact, not even Ashleigh Jarvis. She knew nothing about it. The driver of the lorry saw her stumble into the road, but with only two or three metres between them she was immediately lost from sight below the level of his windscreen, and by then it was too late.

Even by standing on the brakes the driver was unable to stop the truck for another twenty metres, and by that time Ashleigh Jarvis was lying bleeding and unconscious in the gutter behind him.

She was no longer hugging herself though, and perhaps that's why she looked as if she had finally fallen apart.

On the other side of the Cadogan Estate Charlie Atkins had his fleece zipped right up to the neck so that it covered his collar and tie. There was nothing he could do to hide the suit trousers and polished shoes below the fleece though; and nothing he could ever say to convince his father that choir practice didn't need Sunday-best clothes. All he could hope was that the darkness would hide what he was wearing if he passed any of the Kaddy Boys on the ten-minute walk to the church.

As yet he hadn't seen anyone, so perhaps this time it

would be okay. But even though he was off the estate, he was still alert – so when he heard the sudden thud and the crack of the shop window fracturing beside him he jumped and instinctively stepped sideways, away.

Even as he did so there was another dull thud, and when Charlie looked he could see that both impacts had been caused by a figure in a hoodie wielding a heavy ball-peen hammer inside the shop. The glass was starred in two places, with longer cracks radiating out from these points, but the window's refusal to shatter was clearly annoying the person on the other side of the glass because he was already bringing the hammer back for a third blow.

This time he put so much effort into the swing that his hood slipped back on his head and, a split second before the glass fractured again, Charlie saw the face of Tyler Smith, contorted with effort and concentration.

Wide-eyed, Charlie was transfixed by the weirdness of the scene. As he stared he became aware of other figures inside the minimart – at least two – and of a general noise of breaking and shouting coming from the open door. For a second he wondered if it was a robbery, but if it was, why was Tyler Smith trying to break the window from the *inside*?

Charlie was still trying to make sense of all this when he realised that Tyler's gaze was now locked on him through the crazed glass. The older boy was mouthing something unintelligible, but for Charlie the threatening gesture of his fist was clear enough – he didn't want to be standing there when Tyler Smith came out of the shop. Quickly, Charlie swung away from the window and started to run.

Two or three minutes later, breathless and heart pounding, he vaulted up the church steps two at a time and fumbled in through the door as the organ swelled and voices rose in a few bars of "Everything I Need".

Reverend Michaels was just inside and he turned at Charlie's sudden entrance.

"Charlie? You been running again? How do you expect to sing for the Lord if you're always out of breath?"

"Sorry, Reverend," Charlie said. "I was— I didn't want to be late."

"Okay, well you'd better take a minute to catch up with yourself, then we'll start properly, okay?"

"Okay," Charlie said. "Thanks."

And as he started along the aisle towards the rest of the choir he was glad to be safely in the one place he knew neither Tyler Smith or any of the other Kaddy Boys would come looking for him.

2.

TAMLIN ROAD
19:09 HRS

Holly Blades was running. She was trying to keep up with PC Oz Sitwell, watching for puddles and kerbs in the darkness, dodging the other people on the pavement, and trying to pay attention to the radio traffic in her earpiece, all at the same time.

"*Delta Mike from Nine-Five. Re Gatemead Road. Confirm one injured party. Teenage female in collision with HGV. Urgent medical attention requested. Over.*"

"*Nine-Five, received. Ambulance service on way. ETA three to four minutes.*"

"*Understood. Three-One-Seven from Nine-Five, location please?*"

A couple of paces ahead Holly saw Oz Sitwell raise a hand to his radio without breaking stride: "Nine-Five from Three-One-Seven. We're on Tamlin Street now, Sarge. Two minutes..."

"*Received. Eight-Three-Two from Nine-Five...*"

Holly stopped listening in order to concentrate on running. Below her uniform beret her ponytail swished against the fabric of her stab vest in time with her strides. Even though she'd been wearing the bulky vest and heavy utility belt almost every day for the last two weeks they still seemed to weigh as much as they had when she'd first put them on. Weren't you supposed to get used to them the more you wore them?

Oz cast a glance back towards her and Holly knew he was checking she was still there. She made an extra effort and pushed harder, catching up with him as they rounded a corner and emerged onto the main road. He hardly seemed to be breathing any faster than normal, but Holly knew he was a regular half-marathon runner, so this was only a jog for him.

"Warmed up yet?" Oz asked with a grin.

"Just a bit," Holly panted. Five minutes ago she'd been complaining about being cold as they walked their patrol across the Cadogan Estate. Not any more.

Oz gestured. "Just down there," he said.

Ahead Holly could see the blue lights of Sergeant Stafford's patrol car. It blocked half the road and there was a long line of stationary cars behind it. Others were just barely crawling past in the opposite direction, out of Weston city centre.

Holly and Oz covered another thirty metres at a run and then Oz put his hand out, slowing them to a jog, then a brisk walking pace for the last few metres. When Holly looked at him quizzically he nodded to the crowd of people ahead.

"Try not to turn up out of breath," he said. "Panics people. Get your breath first, then you can ask questions, yeah?"

Holly nodded. "Right."

"Okay, go on then." He gestured her to go first.

Holly hesitated. She couldn't even see over the crowd and

although her uniform made her look bigger than she was, she'd have much preferred just to follow in Oz's six-foot-two wake. But she was out in front now and, with Oz waiting, there was little choice but to go for it.

"Excuse me! Stand back please," Holly called out, trying to sound as convincing as she could. "Stand *back* please!"

For a moment nothing happened, but then a man at the rear of the crowd looked round, saw the two officers and stepped aside. A woman did the same and then, miraculously, the crowd was parting.

Perhaps they only saw the uniform, Holly thought – not the sixteen year old inside it – but she couldn't help feeling a pleasing sense of authority as she carved her way to the front of the crowd. And then she saw the broken figure in the road and the pleasure evaporated in an instant.

The girl was lying on the tarmac, shielded from the traffic by the patrol car. A foil survival blanket was draped over her body and Sergeant Eddie Stafford was kneeling beside her, one hand pressing a wound dressing to her arm, the other making sure her head didn't move. There was blood trickling slowly from the girl's nose and ear, but for some reason what drew Holly's attention most were the two bare feet she could see protruding from the survival blanket.

"Sarge...?" Holly said, uncertain what to do now.

Stafford looked up, first at Holly, then at Oz. When he spoke it was to Oz and his tone was urgent but calm.

"We need to get the ambulance through," he said and

nodded towards the traffic. "See if you can shift that lot and get it in, okay?"

"Got it," Oz said and went off to deal with the vehicles.

Stafford looked to Holly.

"Anyone else here yet?"

"No, Sarge. I haven't seen anyone."

"Okay, come here."

Stafford was in his late forties with short-cropped, greying hair. He had a reputation for being tough but fair – maybe tougher than he was fair when it came to Trainee Police Officers like Holly – but at least you knew he was the real thing: still on the street after nearly thirty years in the Job.

"Have you dealt with an injured person before?" Stafford asked as Holly moved closer.

"Yes, Sarge. Sort of."

The "sort of" was an old lady who'd tripped on some steps and gashed her knee in the fall. All Holly had done was apply a gauze pad to the bleeding and stay with the woman till the ambulance came. This was different though, and Holly knew it.

"Right, come round here then," Stafford said. "Kneel down."

Holly did as she was told. When she was in position, Stafford took her hand and placed it on the wound dressing on the girl's arm. "Press there, keep the pressure on. Use your other hand to stabilise her head. Don't let it move, okay?"

"Yes, Sarge."

"Right."

Stafford straightened up with a grunt and stepped away, moving immediately to deal with the crowd of onlookers and speak to the man who was sitting on the kerb some metres away: the driver of the lorry.

Holly looked down at the girl's face. Her skin was pale, almost grey, and streaked with make-up. A purple-pink swelling from the collision was already distorting her cheekbone and right eye.

What was she? Holly wondered. Thirteen? Fourteen, maybe? She seemed very frail, very damaged and only the weak bubbling of blood at her nostril gave any sign that she was still breathing.

"It's all right," Holly said to the girl. "My name's Holly. You'll be okay."

Then, in the distance, she heard the two-tone siren of an ambulance. It was getting closer.

"That's the ambulance," Holly told the girl. "They'll be here soon. Don't worry."

On the damp tarmac the girl didn't move.

3

Drew Alford saw them coming as they rounded the corner of the tower block, still running but only at a jog now. None of the gang was what you'd call fit and they'd run all the way from the minimart, a good quarter of a mile.

Skank and Rizza were both pretty light, but Tyler Smith – bigger and heavier than either of them – was down to a fast walk. As soon as he saw Alford he slowed and then stopped altogether, breathing hard from the unaccustomed exertion.

"All right?" Alford asked as he came closer. "How'd it go?"

Skank had a grin on his face.

"Nah, no problem," Rizza said. "Piece of piss."

"You didn't say nothing, right – to the owner?"

Skank shook his head, still grinning. He was a skinny, grubby-looking figure with acne and about a dozen whiskers on his chin. "Didn't need to," he said. "You shoulda seen his face when we start tipping stuff over. Then Ty does the windows and the woman's all screaming: '*Don't do that! Don't do that! I know what you want!*'"

"Where's the hammer?" Alford asked, turning to Tyler.

"Here," Tyler said and showed him the hammer concealed under his hoodie.

"Okay, stash it somewhere in case we need it again."

Alford looked at his watch, thought for a moment, then addressed them all. "Okay, anyone asks, we were all down Jak's offie from quarter past six. I went in for the fags then we stayed round the side, okay? Hanging out."

"You an' all?" Tyler asked.

"Course me an' all," Alford said irritably. "That way we all say the same thing, dickhead."

Tyler scowled at the insult but said nothing else.

"So what you want to do now?" Skank asked, hunching into his coat. Now that they'd stopped running and the adrenalin rush was evaporating he was starting to feel the chill.

"You can do what you want," Alford said. "I'm going in. It's too fucking cold to hang about here any more. Tomorrow, though, right? I'll text you."

"Okay," Skank said. "I might get a burger, down Patrick's." He nudged Rizza. "You wanna come?"

"Sure, whatever," Rizza said.

"Stay away from the minimart," Alford warned them as they turned to move off.

"What about you?" he asked Tyler as the others walked away.

Tyler shrugged. "Dunno," he said. "If you're going home I could walk back with you."

"All right, come on then," Alford said.

Together they headed towards the looming shape of Penrice House, the windows of its fifteen storeys lit yellow in the cold winter's night sky. As they crossed the road towards it Tyler said: "So how much we gonna get?"

"For what?"

"You know – for doing the shop."

"Say it a bit louder," Alford said. "Tell everyone."

Tyler glanced quickly along the road and realised they were alone. He scowled then because he hated it when Drew made him look stupid.

"So how much?" he asked again.

"I dunno yet. Depends, don't it?"

"What if he doesn't give us anything?"

"He will. Anyway, it's not about that."

"What do you mean? I thought—"

"It was a try-out," Alford said. "Prove he can take us seriously. After this there's gonna be more. *That's* where we're gonna be earning for real."

He glanced at Tyler – never the brightest of bulbs – to see if he'd got it, but from the uncertain look on Tyler's face it was clear he was still struggling with the idea.

"Never mind," Alford told him. "Let me worry about that. Just remember what I said. We were all down the offie, right? All of us."

"Yeah, I know," Tyler said.

"Right. Come on then, let's get a fucking move on before the cops think about looking to see who's around."

And with that he shoved his hands in his pockets and quickened their pace towards the entrance to the tower block.

4.

GATEMEAD ROAD
19:16 HRS

The paramedics had arrived two or three minutes ago and, doing as she'd been told, Holly continued to hold the wound dressing in place on the girl's arm while they did their job. One of the paramedics – a woman in her thirties called Blanche – was carefully fitting a neck support to stabilise the girl's head. The other, named Sancho, was monitoring the girl's stats with a stethoscope in his ears.

"BP's one-twenty over sixty," he said. "Pulse weak – you on apprenticeship then?" He glanced over at Holly so she'd know he was talking to her.

"A trainee, yeah," Holly nodded. Like all the other TPOs she hated being called an apprentice. She thought it made them sound less official, but the label had stuck when the TPO scheme was announced and that was how most people thought of them: apprentice coppers.

"Shallow breath sounds on the right. Query pneumothorax," Sancho said to Blanche. Then: "First RTC?"

"What? Oh. First serious one, yeah," Holly said. It still struck her as odd, the way all emergency service personnel jumped in and out of banter mode, no matter how serious the situation.

Sancho nodded. "Don't worry," he said. "This isn't so bad.

If she'd gone under the wheels you'd be on shovel duty by now."

"Knock it off, Sancho," Blanche said, gruffly. She had finished fixing the neck support and was straightening up. "Ignore him, love," she said to Holly. "Everyone knows we don't use shovels."

"Right," Holly said.

"Nah – it's wallpaper scrapers."

Sancho chuckled at the gag and Holly knew she'd have to let that one go. TPOs were fair game as far as the police regs were concerned, and now that seemed to extend to the paramedics as well.

When Blanche went off to get a spinal board, Sancho changed position. "Let me have a look at her arm," he said.

Holly moved her hand from the wound dressing and Sancho gently peeled it off. The flesh of the upper arm was sliced down to the yellow of the bone, but there was remarkably little blood: just a bit of oozing now that the pressure had been released.

"Not too bad," Sancho said. "She'll have a nice scar. But that'll be the least of her worries."

"Is—" Holly hesitated. "Will she be okay?" It was the question she'd been waiting to ask since the paramedics had arrived.

Sancho seemed to register the fact that Holly was genuine in her concern and treated it seriously.

"Once we get her stabilised she'll be fine," he said, strangely definite in his words.

He took a fresh dressing from the kit beside him and leaned a little closer to Holly, lowering his voice. "Best to remember there's always a chance the victim still knows what's going on around them," he said. "Even like this. Best to stay positive."

Holly nodded, matching his whisper. "So she isn't...?"

"She could have a fractured skull, and her vitals aren't great. We'll see. You want to check her pockets, see if she's got any ID?"

"Is that okay?"

"Yeah, go ahead."

The only pockets Holly could find were in the cardigan the girl was wearing. In the left-hand one she found a small leather purse, but before she could open it Blanche returned with the spinal board, and when the two paramedics started the procedure to move the girl Holly stood up and backed out of the way.

For the first time since she'd arrived, Holly looked round. Apart from Oz and Sergeant Stafford there were two more uniformed regs in attendance now and the crowd of onlookers had been moved back from the roadside. Under their gaze Holly suddenly felt exposed, and because she wasn't sure what else to do now she opened the girl's purse to look inside. There were a few loose coins and a laminated bus pass. The photo it carried wasn't very good but it was clearly the injured girl. Her name was printed underneath: Ashleigh Jarvis.

"All right, Holly?" Sergeant Stafford had approached while she was still looking at the bus pass.

"Yes, Sarge," she said, trying to make it sound as positive as she could. "I found some ID. Her name's Ashleigh Jarvis."

She handed the purse and bus pass to Stafford who looked at them, then nodded. "Good. Means we can find her family. She'll be going to the Vic, so I want you to go with her in the ambulance. I'll send a reg down as soon as I can but we need to deal with the scene. All you have to do is stay on hand and if there's any significant change in her condition let me know, okay?"

"Yes, Sarge," Holly said.

The stretcher was in the ambulance now and as Blanche closed one of the back doors she called out: "Eddie?" She was ready to go.

Stafford looked, then gave a wave. He turned back to Holly. "Okay – gob shut, ears open, and don't get in their way. Got it?"

"Yes, Sarge," Holly said, and she ran to get in the ambulance.

5

"Yeah, it's me," Drew Alford said into his phone as he emerged from the stairwell. He was alone now. Tyler lived two floors below.

"That thing you wanted. It's done... Nah, it was fine, we just did what you said... Yeah... When? ... Okay, I'll see you then."

He rang off as he reached the third door along the landing and took a worn Yale key from his pocket. He shoved it into the lock and twisted, pushing the door open as he did so.

Inside the flat Alford looked into the sitting room, then the double bedroom. Both were empty as he'd known they would be as soon as he'd walked in and not heard the telly. Gone down the pub, probably. Well that was okay. It suited him.

In the kitchen he went to the washing machine and squatted down to look inside. There was a pile of wet laundry in the drum, washed but not spun. He thought about it for a beat, then opened the door and pulled the damp clothes out onto the cracked vinyl floor.

Standing up, he stripped off the clothes he was wearing, pushing each item into the machine as he took it off: trainers, socks, jeans, T-shirt, hoodie. He put his mobile, fags, lighter and a small amount of loose change on the worktop.

When he was down to his pants he searched the cluttered and untidy worktop for the washing powder and couldn't find it. He swore, then squatted and searched the cupboards underneath, finally locating the box under the sink.

Without measuring he poured powder into the dispenser drawer of the washing machine and rammed it home. Then he took off his pants, chucked them in with the rest of his clothes and set the machine to its highest and longest setting. For a moment nothing happened, but then there was a click and a hum and the sound of water under pressure.

Alford waited there, naked, until he was sure that water was filling the drum, then he padded barefoot to the bathroom and turned on the shower. The spray head was old and only half the jets worked. While he waited for the water to warm up he looked at himself in the mirror.

He examined his lean body from different angles, checking that there were no marks. He'd been pretty sure there wouldn't be, but it was as well to make certain.

To his own eye he reckoned he had a good body; pretty bloody decent. So it was just a shame it'd had to be that way. She didn't know what she'd missed. Fucking shame.

He chuckled when he realised he'd made a pun and turned away from the mirror. The shower was making steam now, so he opened the door of the cabinet and stepped inside. Then he started to wash himself down. Thoroughly.

6.

STARLIGHT MINIMART
FIRSLEY ROAD
19:19 HRS

Inside the minimart, TPO Sam Marsden examined the three starburst fractures in the window. It was hard to believe that none of them had actually smashed through the glass but only filled it with jagged cracks.

Turning to look at the rest of the shop, Sam thought it looked as if some kind of natural disaster had struck – a hurricane, maybe. There was an acrid smell of vinegar from a broken bottle and down both aisles the contents of shelves and racks were strewn across the floor. At the far end of the shop the wife of the owner, Mrs Walker, was bending down to pick up tins, placing them back on the nearest shelves, seemingly at random.

Now that he'd seen the full extent of the damage, Sam picked his way carefully back through the spilled crisps and packets of biscuits towards the till where PC Yvonne Dunlop was talking to the owner. Yvonne was in her early thirties, as tall as Sam, with high cheekboned good looks. It was as well not to be distracted by that though. Yvonne Dunlop had a reputation for telling it like it was and she didn't take shit from anyone.

"What about the CCTV, Mr Walker?" she said, and gestured to the camera attached to the ceiling above the counter.

The shop owner shook his head. “Doesn't work. It's just a dummy.”

“Right. Well, maybe you should think about getting the real thing. It might help prevent something like this happening again.”

“You know how much it costs to put that in? Be about two months' profits. We might as well pack up now.”

“You've had trouble before though, right? Just after Christmas?”

Mr Walker nodded, but it seemed to Sam that there was some reluctance to the admission.

“So was this the same people?”

“I dunno, do I?” the man said. “They had hoods – hoodies – I couldn't see who they were.”

Yvonne made a note. “Any idea how old?”

“Teenagers.”

“White, black, Asian?”

“I dunno. White, I think – look, I told you, it was all too fast to tell. One minute there's nothing, then the next they're steaming in, shouting and yelling, stuff going all over the place...”

“Did they speak to you? Did they demand money or try to get into the till?”

“No, nothing like that. They just wanted to trash the place. One of them had a hammer and he went straight for the window.”

Yvonne paused in her writing, then looked directly at the

shopkeeper. "So why would they do that do you think? Why would they want to trash the place rather than try and take anything?"

For a moment it seemed as if Mr Walker might say something about that, but only for a moment, then he shook his head. "I dunno. Look, it's kids, right? Probably think it's a laugh or something."

"You haven't had anyone making threats, demanding money?"

"No."

"You sure? Cos to me it looks like that's what this might be about."

Mr Walker shook his head again, resolute. "No, nothing like that."

Yvonne held his gaze for a moment longer, then let it go. "Okay," she said. "We'll need statements from both you and your wife."

"I'll get her," Mr Walker said and moved out from behind the counter as if he was glad of the excuse to leave.

Yvonne watched him go, her expression less than impressed, then she turned to Sam. "You can take Mrs Walker's statement. She's not going to tell you any more than her husband so don't waste any more time than you have to. It's going to end up as NFA whatever."

NFA was No Further Action and Sam was coming to realise that it was a common fact of life in a lot of cases like this: small scale, no arrests.

"I don't get it," he said. "I mean, why bother to report it if they don't want to tell us anything?"

"Insurance," Yvonne said flatly. "Can't claim unless they've got a case number."

"So you think they *do* know who it was?"

"Maybe not who the youths were, but I'd bet they know who sent them. They're not going to say though, cos that'd only make things worse." She gestured at the dummy CCTV camera. "Even a real one of those doesn't stop someone trashing the place, so what're you going to spend your money on – CCTV or the guy who can stop it happening in the first place?"

Before Sam could frame an answer his radio came to life. It was Sergeant Stafford's voice. "*Six-One-Four from Nine-Five, receiving?*"

"Six-One-Four, go ahead."

"*How long before you finish at your current location?*"

Sam looked to Yvonne for guidance.

"Ten minutes," she said.

"Nine-Five, we'll be free in ten minutes," Sam told Stafford.

"*Okay, soon as you are I need someone for a notification of an accident and a ride to the Vic. Name of Jarvis.*"

7.

EMERGENCY DEPT
QUEEN VICTORIA HOSPITAL
19:43 HRS

Holly had almost had to run to keep up with the paramedics as they wheeled the stretcher from the ambulance into the ED. She'd caught bits of the rapid-fire exchange of medical terminology between the hospital staff who swooped in as soon as they entered the building, but it was too fast and too full of abbreviations to make sense of. All she did know was that Ashleigh Jarvis's condition hadn't improved on the fifteen minute, siren-wailing journey to the Queen Victoria Hospital.

And again – because she'd been following the stretcher – Holly had noticed the girl's bare feet. Something about them wasn't right, but for a moment she couldn't work out what. Then she'd realised: they were dirty. It was possible that the girl had lost her shoes when the truck hit her, but if so, why were the soles of her feet so dirty – as if she'd been walking barefoot *before* the accident?

When the stretcher bumped through the doors into Resus Holly was left outside, but she watched through the window as Ashleigh was transferred from stretcher to exam table. A doctor shone a torch in the unconscious girl's eyes, but he had to hold her eyelids back to do it. Then a nurse pulled a screen into place and that was it: show over.

A few moments later Blanche and Sancho came out of Resus. Blanche was on her radio but Sancho spotted Holly and came over to where she was standing.

"That's us," he said cheerfully. "Hump and dump."

"So what'll happen to her now?" Holly asked.

Sancho shrugged. "They'll do an assessment, get her stabilised and decide on treatment. They'll probably want a CT scan to see how bad the head injury is too."

"Is she still unconscious?"

Sancho nodded. "Don't think you'll be talking to her today."

"Sanch?" Blanche called along the corridor. "Possible stroke at Stockton."

"'Kay." Sanch waved and to Holly he said: "I was you, I'd get a drink and have a sit down while you've got a chance. Grab it while you can. See you later."

And then he was off.

Once the paramedics were gone Holly felt that her only real connection to the case had been cut. No one else would know that she'd ridden in with Ashleigh, or that Sergeant Stafford had told her to keep him updated. It left her feeling unsure about exactly what to do next, so after another glance through the window she moved to sit on a red plastic chair with a view of the Emergency Department doors.

From her stab vest she took out a pen and a green pocketbook, found her last entry and then started to write below it. This wasn't an official record – anything that might be called on as evidence had to go in a different, red book – but this pocketbook was part of her practical assessment. What she wrote here would be reviewed by her college tutors as part of the process of showing that she was capable of seeing and recording pertinent details of the situations she came across on patrol.

Under the date, time and location she wrote:

Attended RTC with PC Sitwell, Gatemead Road. Sgt Stafford i/c.

Victim: teenage female (13-14?). Unconscious. Head injury, laceration to arm. Struck by lorry. Driver present at scene.

Possible victim ID = Ashleigh Jarvis. Bus pass + purse in pocket.

Weston Ambulance Service attended. Accompanied victim to Queen Victoria Hosp. Still unconscious at 19:45.

She paused, trying to think of anything else and when she did, she hesitated before writing it. But in the end she added: *Victim has no shoes. Feet dirty.*

Then the door to Resus opened and the doctor who'd examined Ashleigh emerged. He headed towards the nurses' station and Holly jumped up to catch him.

"Doctor...?"

The doctor looked round and Holly caught up.

"Doctor, I'm TPO Blades from Morningstar Road Station. I came in with the female victim of the RTC. Can you tell me how she is?"

The doctor looked her over. He was about thirty-five, tall, with a thin face. "Is there another officer with you?" he asked, glancing round.

"I'm waiting for someone else to arrive, but my sergeant asked me to keep him updated. Can you tell me how she's doing?"

The doctor ignored the question. "You're a trainee you said?"

"Yes, but—"

The doctor shook his head. "Her condition could be life-threatening so I think you'd better get a regular officer to come in. Ask a nurse to page me when they arrive: Dr Scobie."

Without waiting for a response he started away and Holly could feel herself flush red. For a moment she almost started back to her seat, but the way he'd dismissed her so casually really rankled, and after a second she pushed back her shoulders and went after him.

"Doctor? – Dr Scobie?"

With a theatrical sigh the doctor paused and half turned. "*Yes?*"

"Sir, just so you know, as a TPO I do have the authority to take statements and request details of an incident from witnesses."

Dr Scobie opened his mouth to speak, but Holly didn't give him the chance. "And under Section 89 of the Police Act, obstructing an officer—"

"Obstructing?" Scobie cut in. "Listen—"

"Please let me finish, sir. Obstructing an officer carries the penalty of imprisonment, a fine or both."

Scobie looked at her incredulously. "Are you saying you're going to *arrest* me?" he said.

"No, sir. I'm just trying to save everyone a lot of wasted time and energy," Holly told him, managing to hold his gaze.

Scobie was still for a beat, but finally he shook his head. "I don't fucking believe it," he said, but this time he didn't turn away. "All right, over there."

He moved across to a quieter section of the corridor, then turned to address Holly as she opened her pocketbook.

"In terms of your accident, she's got a laceration to her upper arm, a tension pneumothorax and a possible subdural haematoma with a base of the neck fracture. We'll know for certain when she's had a scan, but if there is a haematoma she'll need an operation as soon as possible to reduce the pressure on her brain and stop the bleeding. We've had to intubate her and her condition's serious, bordering on critical."

"Okay," Holly said, writing quickly to keep up. "Is there anything else?"

"Yes. From the initial exam I think it's possible she may also have been sexually assaulted."

"Sorry?" Holly stopped writing and looked up. "Why?"

"She wasn't wearing any pants when she was brought in and she's got some bruises and grazes round her thighs and pubic area which aren't consistent with being knocked down. My recommendation would be to ask your Forensic

Medical Examiner to come in and carry out a rape exam – okay?"

"Yes. Thank you." Holly thought rapidly. "What about her clothes?"

"They'll be bagged for evidence, but I'm not handing them over to a trainee."

"No, that's fine. Thank you. I'll let my sergeant know."

"Right. Can I go now?" His voice was heavy with sarcasm. "Or will I be arrested?"

"No, sir. Thank you for your help," Holly said politely.

As the doctor turned away he was shaking his head. "Un-fucking-believable," he muttered.

For a moment after he'd gone Holly continued to write down everything he'd said, then she keyed her radio. "Delta Mike Nine-Five from Seven-Six-Two, free to speak?"

After a moment, Sergeant Stafford's voice came over her earpiece. "*Go ahead, Holly.*"

"Sarge, I've got an update on the condition of the RTC victim."

"*How is she?*"

"Serious or critical, Sarge, but there's something else. The doctor who examined her thinks she might have been sexually assaulted. He thinks we should get the FME down here."

She waited for a beat and then Stafford's voice came back, serious. "*I'll have someone with you asap. Nine-Five out.*"

8.

MAYBERRY COURT
19:51 HRS

Sam Marston had grown up on the outskirts of a small West Country town where the tallest building was a department store with three floors. That hundreds of people could live on top of each other in a place like Mayberry Court was still an alien concept to him, although it was a very real fact. True, this block didn't have quite as bad a reputation as the Cadogan Estate, just across the main road, but the graffiti, litter and the smell of piss in darker corners told you all you needed to know. No one did foot patrol in either place on their own.

"Don't take any notice of what they say or do at first, okay? Just let me deal with it."

Sam could tell from her tone that Yvonne was dead serious about this. "Okay," he said. Then: "Why? – I mean, what do you *think* they'll do?"

Yvonne shook her head. "Can't tell. A copper turns up on your doorstep, it's usually bad news. Then you tell them the last thing in the world they want to hear. Sometimes they laugh because they can't believe it; sometimes they just go quiet."

"Laugh?" Sam found this hard to believe.

"It's just shock – least she's not dead, that's something. Anyway, just be aware."

They left the stairs and headed along the walkway, Yvonne checking door numbers. Most of the windows they passed had the curtains closed against the night. It was the time when most people would be settling down for the evening; having dinner, putting the telly on, glad they didn't have to go out in the dark and the cold. Except now someone would have to: that was why they were here.

At a blue door with a brass number 23 on it, Yvonne stopped. She gave it a second then knocked on the door just below the spyhole. There was no bell.

A few seconds passed, then the door opened and a woman with bleach-blonde hair and dark brown roots looked out at them. She had a slightly pinched look, with heavy make-up round her eyes. "Yes?" she said.

"I'm sorry to disturb you," Yvonne said. "Are you Mrs Jarvis – Dee Jarvis?"

"Yes," the woman said. "What's happened?"

"I'm PC Dunlop, this is TPO Marsden. It's about Ashleigh. Do you think we could come in for a moment?"

The woman frowned, glanced at Sam, then back to Yvonne. "What's happened?" she asked again.

"It'd be better if we could talk inside. Can we?"

Mrs Jarvis was still for a moment, then nodded and stepped back so they could enter. Yvonne motioned to Sam and went in, taking off her cap as she did so. Sam pulled off his beret and rolled it up.

In the sitting room Mrs Jarvis picked up a packet of

cigarettes and a lighter. The television was on and there was an ironing board set up so that she could watch as she ironed.

"What's it about?" Mrs Jarvis asked, lighting a cigarette. "Is she in trouble – Ash?"

"No, not like that," Yvonne said. "Maybe you'd better sit down."

The woman shook her head. "I'm all right. What is it?" But even as she said it Sam could see her hand start to tremble.

Yvonne took a second, then said: "I'm afraid there's been an accident. A girl was injured on Gatemead Road earlier and from the ID she was carrying we think she may be Ashleigh."

"No," Mrs Jarvis said, definitely. "No, Ash is on her way home from her mate's – Lauren. She texted me."

"When was that?"

"I dunno. A bit ago."

She moved to a coffee table and picked up her phone. After a moment she said, "It was twenty to seven. She said 'Home soon. Might get chips first tho.' – See?"

She held up the phone, as if it was proof that Yvonne was wrong.

"I'm sorry," Yvonne said. "We're pretty sure that it's Ashleigh who was knocked down. She's been taken to the Queen Victoria, but her condition *is* serious. We'd like to take you down there."

"No!" the woman said again – harder, angrier. "You've got it wrong. It's not Ash. She'll be home any minute."

"Mrs Jarvis..." Yvonne began.

But even as she said it Sam saw the anger in Dee Jarvis's face begin to dissolve and then she was sobbing, tears welling in her eyes. "No," she said, almost in a whimper. "No, not Ash. Not Ash..."

9.

EMERGENCY DEPT.
QUEEN VICTORIA HOSPITAL
20:10 HRS

"You watch, CID'll come in – they're bound to for a rape."

Holly said nothing. Apart from the fact that she didn't like the know-it-all way Sam Marsden always reckoned to be one step ahead of everyone else, she was more interested in watching Ashleigh's mother as she spoke to Dr Scobie. Sergeant Stafford and Yvonne Dunlop were on either side of her, saying nothing.

"Her mum said she'd been at a friend's house," Sam went on. "So if she was on her way home when she was attacked we could be on door-to-door – see if anyone saw her on the way, if she was with anyone."

Finally Holly looked at him. "How do you know she wasn't assaulted at the friend's house *before* she left?" she said flatly.

"She's a girl – the friend. Name's Lauren."

"Doesn't mean someone else wasn't there as well though, does it?"

"No. Maybe," Sam said, grudgingly.

She was right, and he was annoyed that he hadn't thought of it, especially since he was the one who wanted to go into

CID eventually. Trouble was, Holly was sharp and she never seemed to have a problem fitting into a situation, whereas Sam still felt awkward and unprepared a lot of the time.

Across the corridor Yvonne Dunlop led Dee Jarvis to a chair, an arm round her waist. It struck Holly as an unusually sympathetic gesture from a PC who'd drop a suspect into an armlock if they gave her any bullshit at all.

"We're going back to Gatemead Road," Stafford said, approaching the two TPOs. "Yvonne's going to stay with Ashleigh's mother for the time being."

"What'll happen now, Sarge?" Sam asked.

"What do you think?" Stafford had a habit of turning a question back on the person who asked it.

"CID will come in because of the sexual assault?"

"*Suspected* assault," Stafford corrected him, but nodded. Then his attention shifted to Holly. "I want a word with you."

He led her aside leaving Sam where he was. Holly could guess what was coming.

"Did you threaten to arrest Dr Scobie?"

"No, Sarge."

Stafford gave her a narrow-eyed look. "He's under the distinct impression that you did."

Holly knew there was no point in trying to play it down. She said, "I told him that obstructing an investigation was an offence and then he asked if I was going to arrest him. I said no."

"In what way was he obstructing an investigation?" Stafford asked. It was impossible to gauge what he was thinking.

"I asked him for an update on Ashleigh's condition but he wouldn't talk to me. He said he'd only talk to a reg."

Stafford chewed that over for a moment, then he said: "So you misled him."

"Not on purpose."

Another look.

"Well, yeah, a bit. But there was no *reason* not to tell me, and if you'd had to send a reg down when you were already busy..."

Stafford raised a hand. "Okay," he said. "I've reminded Dr Scobie that good communications help everyone, so in future I don't think there'll be a problem."

Holly didn't think there would either, not if Stafford had done the reminding.

"But just remember," Stafford went on, "you're not the only person who comes in here needing information or help. If someone's pissed off with you, they're liable to carry it over to anyone else in a uniform. Got it?"

"Yes, Sarge."

"Right." He gave her a last hawkish look, then turned away. "Sam?"

From where he'd been watching the exchange, Sam came across.

"You asked Mrs Jarvis about Ashleigh's movements and the clothes she was wearing, right?"

"Yes, Sarge," Sam said. They'd asked the questions on the way to the hospital.

"Okay, update Holly on the way back to Gatemead Road. DS Woods should be there by the time we are. Holly will be briefing him."

"Me?" Holly was taken by surprise.

"You," Stafford said.

"Yes, Sarge."

Was that a punishment or a test to see how well she'd cope – or maybe both? But before Holly had time to figure it out Stafford was gesturing brusquely for them to move. "Come on, then. Prove you can walk and chew gum at the same time."

10.

GATEMEAD ROAD
20:24 HRS

"The victim is Ashleigh Jarvis. She's fourteen and lives at 23 Mayberry Court with her mother, Dee Jarvis. Father absent for some time."

Holly glanced up from her notebook to see if this was what DS Woods wanted to hear. She only knew him by sight and he hadn't looked particularly overjoyed to discover that Holly would be briefing him, although he hadn't complained either. He was a solid-looking man, early forties, with an unexcitable manner. He was wearing a bulky waterproof jacket over his suit and he also had a cold.

"Go on," he said, seemingly more interested in finding a tissue to blow his nose than in what Holly was saying.

Holly looked back at her notes. Verbal briefings were on the monthly assessment list but she hadn't had to give one "live" before.

"According to her mother, Ashleigh was at a friend's house – Lauren Booth, 165 Escott Road. At about 18:40 Mrs Jarvis got a text from Ashleigh to say she'd be home soon and at 19:06 the RTC was reported by a member of the public."

"Have you got a description of the clothes Ashleigh was wearing when she went out?"

"Yes, sir. Apart from what she was wearing when she was knocked down, her mother says she had a dark green coat with a hood. She also had a bag – Indian design. We didn't find either of them at the scene."

"Right. Thanks," DS Woods said. He turned to Stafford. "How certain are they that she was sexually assaulted?"

"Her knickers are missing, there are scratches on her thighs… Pretty sure. The mother's given her consent for a rape exam, so…"

Woods sniffed and thought about it. "It'd only take her about five minutes to walk from Escott Road to here if she came through the estate, so that leaves about twenty minutes unaccounted for. Also means we're looking at the estate as a possible location. That's going to be fun in the dark."

"Sir?" Holly said.

The two sergeants looked at her. Holly hesitated, then said: "When Ashleigh was in the ambulance I noticed she didn't have any shoes. And her feet were dirty. I mean, they were really dirty – like she'd walked or run quite a way without anything on them."

"Any shoes recovered on the road?" Woods asked Stafford.

Stafford shook his head. "No."

"Okay," Woods said to Holly. "I'll keep it in mind. Thanks." He turned back to Stafford. "How many bodies have we got?"

"Just who's here, including the TPOs," Stafford said. "They're supposed to be going off but I can assign them for a couple more hours."

"Okay," Woods said. "If you can look after the search, I'll go and see this friend of Ashleigh's, find out what she knows – okay if I take Miss Blades in case the girl's on her own?"

"You all right with that?" Stafford asked Holly. "Any reason you need to get back to the Section House?"

"No, Sarge, I'm fine," Holly said, trying not to sound too pleased at the assignment.

"Okay, I'll entrust you to DS Woods's tender mercies. Know what I'm going to say next?"

Holly nodded. "Gob and ears, Sarge."

"Right."

11.

BOOTH RESIDENCE
ESCOTT ROAD
20:43 HRS

"Can you remember what time Ashleigh left here?" DS Woods asked.

On the sofa Lauren Booth sat with her hands wedged between her thighs, as if she didn't trust them not to shake if she removed them. She still seemed to be in shock from the news about Ashleigh and her mother had put a comforting arm round her shoulder.

"Just after six," Lauren said dully. "We'd been watching telly."

Holly saw Woods frown. He looked to Lauren's father. "Is that what you remember? Six o'clock?"

"I don't know," Mr Booth said. He was about forty, and was standing by the fireplace. "I went out about ten to six. She was still here when I left."

"It *was* about six," Mrs Booth said. "I asked her if she wanted to stay for tea but she said no."

"Okay." Woods made a note, then looked back at her daughter. "Lauren, do you know if Ashleigh was intending to meet anyone on her way home?"

Lauren shook her head. "She was just going home."

But there was something about the way she said it – just the faint hint of a hesitation before she spoke – that struck Holly as not quite right. She glanced at Woods and when he met her eye – just for a second – she knew he'd picked up on it, too.

"She didn't say she'd be stopping off anywhere?" Woods asked Lauren without missing a beat.

Lauren shook her head. "No."

"Why's that matter anyway?" Lauren's father said then. "I mean, if she was knocked down..."

"We think there might be a bit more to it than that," Woods said. "It's possible Ashleigh might have been assaulted before the accident."

"You mean she was mugged or something?" Lauren's mother said, the note in her voice indicating it was almost too terrible a thing to contemplate.

"We're not sure of the details yet, but her bag is missing."

"It's that bloody estate," Mr Booth said. "I won't let Laurie go across it. They're all like wild dogs – 'specially the boys. You can see them, always hanging around on the corners." He gestured off towards the window. "*I* wouldn't walk across there in the dark," he said for emphasis.

DS Woods nodded. "Well, like I said, we're not sure what happened, but it would be helpful to know who Ashleigh's other friends are – anyone she might have seen or talked to on the way home." He looked at Lauren. "Could you tell Holly do you think?"

"I suppose," Lauren said.

"Great." Woods looked to her parents. "I'd like to get a few more details from you, so would it be all right if they used the kitchen to talk?"

"It's a bit of a mess," Mrs Booth said apologetically.

"Don't worry," Holly said, taking her cue from the DS. "Can't be any worse than ours."

She stood up and waited for Lauren to do the same – which she did, but without any enthusiasm.

Holly followed Lauren to the kitchen and closed the door behind them. As she did so Lauren turned to her directly, her face troubled and confused. "How badly hurt is she – really?" she asked.

"It is pretty serious," Holly said, being careful not to say any more than DS Woods had already. She took out her pocketbook – the red one – and sat down at the small kitchen table.

"From the accident or...or from being mugged?"

"Mostly from the accident," Holly said.

"Will I be able to see her? If I go to the hospital?"

"I think it'd be better to wait till tomorrow and call to find out. Her mum's with her though."

Lauren shook her head as if it was all too hard to take in. She sat down on a chair. "I can't believe she's...that it's happened, you know? Just like that. She was here, we were watching TV and then..."

Holly nodded to show she understood. "Does Ashleigh come round here a lot after school?"

"Yeah, I suppose. Sometimes I go to hers. Dad doesn't like

that as much though. He always comes to pick me up."

"Because of the estate?"

Lauren nodded.

"But Ashleigh's mum's all right about her going home on her own?"

Lauren shook her head. "She doesn't like it either. But she can't do anything about it – they don't have a car." She glanced towards the sitting room. "Dad should've taken her. I wanted him to, before he went out."

Holly frowned. "Why? I mean, was there a reason why you wanted him to give her a lift today?"

"No," Lauren said. "He just could've, that's all."

Abruptly she stood up again and went over to the sink to run water into a mug.

"I hate it. I hate living round here," Lauren said, turning back with the mug in her hand. "Crappy school, crappy shops, crappy everything."

And then Holly knew for certain that Lauren was covering something. Changing the conversation like that was the sort of tactic she might have used to dodge questions from her mum.

"Listen, Lauren, this is important," Holly said. "Was Ashleigh all right when she left here? Was there anything wrong?"

"No, I just said, didn't I?" Lauren's mouth set firm against giving anything else. "She was fine. I don't– No. She was fine."

Holly took a beat. "Okay," she said in the end. "Can you tell me the names of anyone else she was friends with?"

* * *

Outside the house a few minutes later DS Woods waited until they'd walked a few steps along the street before he said anything. In the meantime he blew his nose morosely.

Holly looked across the road towards the blocks of flats that rose in the darkness from the Cadogan Estate. Many of their windows were lit, but where the surrounding, lower buildings crowded in there were patches of darkness – areas that couldn't be made out – and a sense that if you went in there you'd better know where you were going and not linger on the way.

"So did you find out what was going on?" Woods asked when he'd finished wiping his nose.

"Not really, sir," Holly said. "She wasn't telling the truth though – I mean, she wasn't telling everything she knows."

Woods sniffed hard. "It's 'Sarge', not 'sir'," he said, but it was a throwaway comment, as if it wasn't important. "So *what* do you think she wasn't telling?"

Holly had been trying to work out the same thing.

"She told me she wanted her dad to give Ashleigh a lift home."

"So?"

"It was the way she said it – like there was a reason – but I couldn't get her to tell me what it was."

Holly was disappointed with her lack of success but Woods didn't appear too worried. "That's teenage girls for you," he said without any trace of irony. "What about Ashleigh's other friends?"

"I got four names – all girls from school – but it didn't seem like they were close friends."

"What about boys then – boyfriends?"

"No. I asked, but Lauren said Ashleigh didn't have one."

"*Ever* had one?"

"No, it didn't sound like it."

"Okay," Woods said, keying the central locking on the car. "Well, at least we know what time she left here."

"It's too early though, isn't it?" Holly said. "When Ashleigh texted her mum at twenty to seven, she made it look like she was only just leaving."

Woods paused with his car door half open and gave her a look.

"You think Lauren and her mother got the time wrong?"

Holly shook her head. "No," she said. "I think Ashleigh didn't want her mum to know where she was."

"Any idea why? – Why do *you* lie to your mum?"

"I don't," Holly said, feeling slightly embarrassed. Then she added: "Not unless I'm doing something I don't think she'd like."

"So what's *that* tell you?" Woods said, and he got into the car.

12.

DRURY HOUSE
CADOGAN ESTATE
20:53 HRS

The beam of the Maglite torch cast moving shadows as Sam shone it into the corners of the stairwell. It illuminated discarded newspapers, chip trays and lager cans. Near his feet there were a couple of small syringes without needles. In other words, nothing.

Sam gave the concrete steps a final sweep of the torchlight, then backed out.

A few metres away PC Bob Mulvey was moving along a row of cars in the marked parking spaces below Drury House. He was shining his own torch between the vehicles in fast, jerky movements. Sam would have taken more time, but Mulvey seemed to be intent on covering the ground as quickly as possible – as if he was in a race and wanted to find the prize before anyone else beat him to it. The prize, of course, was the coat, shoes or bag belonging to Ashleigh Jarvis.

"Oi, copper. Lost your truncheon?"

The mocking shout came from high up on one of the balconies and ended in a laugh. Sam looked up but couldn't see anyone. That far away, the owner of the taunting voice knew he was safe.

The cold wind and the renewed threat of rain had cleared the streets and paths around the Cadogan Estate of all but a few people, none of whom came near as Sam quickened his pace to catch up with Mulvey. The PC was near the corner of the parking area now and, as Sam approached he gave the area a last cursory sweep with his torch before switching it off.

"Nothing here," Mulvey said. "We'll try round there." He gestured to the corner of a wall which hid the service area for the flats and started off towards it without waiting for Sam.

Mulvey wasn't a Trainer PC like Yvonne Dunlop, and Sam had only been assigned to him for the duration of this search, but he already disliked the PC's bossy, dismissive manner. A lot of regs didn't rate the TPO scheme very highly, but at least most of them would act as if the TPOs were sixteen and not six.

Flicking his torch on again, Sam ran it along the base of the wall as they moved. The brickwork was covered with dozens of graffiti tags, some harder to decipher than others, but one of the most common was *KB* in large block letters: Kaddy Boys. That was the gang you heard of most often when there was trouble on the Cadogan Estate.

Sam followed Mulvey around the wall to the rear of the tower block – a place of power plants, ventilation systems, bin stores and maintenance sheds. There was an overflowing skip and a council storage container in one corner, illuminated by a single street light. All the lamps on the walls had been smashed.

"Okay," Mulvey said. "You start in there." He gestured to a

bin shelter. "I'll work round to meet you from over there." And with that he headed off towards the skip.

Being away from Mulvey was fine with Sam. He raised his torch and carried it the way the other coppers did – gripped just behind the lens, handle resting on his shoulder so it could be swung down easily in self defence if necessary. Its weight was a comforting reassurance as he moved into the poorly lit entrance to the bin shelter.

The place smelled of rotting food and some things far worse, despite the cold weather. There was litter strewn underfoot and the light of the torch showed four commercial refuse bins, all taller than Sam was. Around them there were a couple of broken TV sets, a Hoover and other abandoned household goods.

Sam took all this in for a moment before moving further into the shelter. He was hidden from Mulvey's sight now and it wasn't a place he wanted to linger, but even so he made himself take time, probing the shadows round the bins with the torch, looking for anything that wasn't just someone else's discarded crap.

He saw the shoe first: black leather, the low-cut sort with a flat heel. It was near a sodden cardboard box and on its own it might have been easy to dismiss as part of the general rubbish. But as he moved closer to get a better look, the light of the torch caught something shiny nearby. And when he redirected the light, Sam saw the brightly coloured fabric and embroidered sequins of a shoulder bag, Indian in design.

His first instinct was to go further forward and pick the thing up, but he caught himself mid-step and stopped. He played the light over the bag one more time to make sure he wasn't seeing things then turned and started away.

Mulvey was looking round the skip twenty metres away when Sam called to him. He looked up, then came across quickly.

"What's up?" he said brusquely.

"In there," Sam nodded. "There's a shoe and a bag – it fits the description we got."

"Show me."

Sam led the way back into the bin shelter, treading more carefully now, then located the shoe and the bag with his torch.

"What do you think?" he asked.

Mulvey stared for a moment. "Have you touched them?"

"No."

"Right. Hold the light there."

Sam did as he was told and Mulvey pulled a blue latex glove onto his right hand, then moved forward. When he got to the bag he squatted, then reached out to gently part the bag's opening and look inside. "There's a mobile," he said.

"So it could be hers."

"Could be."

He left the bag as it was and straightened up. "Did you see anything else?"

"No, just that and the shoe."

"Okay, I'll call it in. Come away."

They came out of the bin shelter and at the entrance Mulvey said, "Stay there," before moving off a few metres to use his radio. Even so, Sam could still hear what he said.

"Nine-Five from Three-Seven-Six, receiving?"

"*Go ahead,*" Stafford's voice came back.

"Yeah, Sarge, I think I might've found the bag," Mulvey said.

13

"Bye, Reverend," Charlie said as he moved down the aisle towards the door of the Baptist church. The other members of the choir – most of them adults – were milling around, putting on coats, chatting. Charlie just wanted to get away.

"Charlie, hold on a second." Reverend Michaels excused himself from the conversation he'd been having with Mrs Johnson and caught up with Charlie. "If you want to wait a few minutes, I can give you a lift home."

"No, thanks, I'm okay," Charlie said. The last thing he needed was to be seen getting out of the Reverend's car in front of the flats. There'd be about a dozen different ways they could use that in school, all of them sick.

"Are you sure? It's not out of my way."

"Yeah, I'm fine. Thanks."

Charlie tried to disengage but it was clear that Reverend Michaels still had something on his mind. "It's good that you still come to choir," he said. "I know a lot of boys your age wouldn't want to. They've got other things to distract them."

"I suppose," Charlie said. It was the only neutral thing he could think of to say.

"It's a shame you can't persuade Ryan to come with you. He's got a good voice."

"He's got a lot of work for exams," Charlie said, knowing full well that this was just a way of dodging the subject.

"The thing is," the Reverend went on, "you seemed a little preoccupied tonight. Is everything all right?"

"Yeah. Yes, it's fine."

"You do know you can come to me with anything that's worrying you, don't you?"

Charlie nodded. "I know. Thank you. But everything's all right."

"Okay. Good," the Reverend said, seeming to accept his word for it at last. "And you're sure you don't want a lift?"

"No, I'm fine," Charlie said. "See you on Sunday."

But as he headed away down the aisle towards the exit he remembered Reverend Michaels's theme for his last sermon: *Do not be a hypocrite before others and keep watch over your lips.*

The thing was, Charlie knew he was a hypocrite. Why else would he say nothing?

Outside, Charlie glanced round as he trotted down the steps, then turned right, uphill. He was still trying to decide which would be the best route to take home – avoiding the minimart of course – when he saw a movement on the corner ahead of him: two figures.

For a moment his heart jumped, already convinced that it was Tyler Smith and another Kaddy Boy lying in wait for him. But even as his feet hesitated between running and stopping he saw the face of the figure nearest to him and felt swift relief. It was Ryan, his brother, and his mate Dav. Both were holding polystyrene chip trays.

"Come on," Ryan called, seeing Charlie's momentary hesitation. "We're bloody freezing waiting for you."

Charlie jogged forward, unable to suppress a grin at the fact that Ryan had decided to come and meet him. He didn't always.

"What you smiling at?" Ryan said when he saw Charlie's face.

"Me? Nothing," Charlie said. "Give us a chip."

14.

DRURY HOUSE
CADOGAN ESTATE
21:02 HRS

Mulvey had moved to stand around the corner from the bin shelter, telling Sam to do the same. He'd said it was because this position was more sheltered from the wind while they waited for the others. But from the way Mulvey lurked in the shadows without speaking, Sam was pretty sure he was hoping that someone would return to the scene of the crime – if this was the scene of the crime – so he could pounce on them.

That'd put the cap on it, Sam thought bitterly. That'd really make Mulvey's day. Not just "I've found the bag", but "I've got a suspect" as well. So Sam said nothing; just stood there and fumed silently.

And then, suddenly, Mulvey tensed and shifted. Sam looked and saw three black kids – two of them older and taller than the other – coming along the rear service road towards them. They didn't seem to be taking much notice of their surroundings, chatting and walking shoulder to shoulder as they ate from chip trays.

"Keep still," Mulvey hissed.

Sam could feel the PC's anticipation as he watched the boys coming closer. And it *did* look as if they might be heading for the bin shelter, or at least going to pass by.

Mulvey let them cross the road and then, when they were only a couple of metres away, he stepped out.

"Stop there, lads. Keep still."

The smaller boy jumped visibly and took a half step back as Mulvey strode quickly towards him. The two older ones reacted but stood their ground.

"What's the problem?" one of them said.

"Just stand still," Mulvey told him, ignoring the question as Sam came and stood to one side. Mulvey's tone was hard and no-nonsense, but more aggressive than it needed to be in Sam's opinion.

"I'm PC Mulvey, this is TPO Marsden. You want to tell us what you're doing here?"

"Going home."

"Which is where?"

"Cloudsley House." He gestured to the block on the east side of the estate. "Why've you stopped us?"

Again Mulvey ignored the question and took out a stop form, then a pen.

"Name?"

"Listen—"

"Name," Mulvey repeated, cutting him off.

Sam knew that Mulvey didn't have the right to be chucking his weight around like this. He also didn't have any right to make them account for themselves if they didn't want to.

The boy took a beat, as if he might argue again, then he said: "Ryan Atkins."

"You?" Mulvey asked the smaller, more nervous boy.

"Charlie Atkins."

"And you?"

"Barclay Davis."

"Right. So where are you coming from?"

"Church," Ryan Atkins said before the lad called Barclay could answer.

Mulvey gave him a look. "Yeah, right."

"Ask Reverend Michaels. Holway Road Baptist. Check it out if you don't believe me."

"Oi! Don't get arsey with me, okay?" Mulvey said sharply. "How long were you there?"

Sam could see the boy's stance stiffening and there was a new note of defiance when he spoke again: "Since seven. We were at choir practice."

"All of you?"

"Yeah."

Sam could tell that Ryan Atkins's growing truculence didn't sit well with Mulvey, but then the PC's attention was taken by a patrol car coming round the corner. It was followed a short distance behind by a second, unmarked car.

Mulvey looked at the vehicles, then decided. "You can finish this off, right?" he said to Sam, handing him the stop form. "NFA."

And before Sam could respond, Mulvey was heading off towards the cars.

Sam watched him go and felt like spitting. Then he looked back to the three lads.

"So can we go now?" Ryan Atkins said.

"Listen," Sam said, trying to engage them. "We think something might have happened round here earlier. If you saw anything..."

"We didn't," Ryan said without hesitation. "We weren't here, I told you. So can we go now or what?"

Sam held his gaze for a second, then looked at the stop form. Mulvey hadn't even entered the date or the time, and if Mulvey couldn't be bothered then Sam didn't see why he should be either. NFA: No Further Action.

"Okay," Sam said. "Sorry to hold you up."

Without even acknowledging that Ryan Atkins nodded to the others and they moved away.

Sam wadded the stop form into a ball and shoved it into his pocket, then turned and headed towards the police cars and the officers around them. He could see Mulvey leading DS Woods into the bin shelter and knew exactly what he'd be saying as he showed him the shoe and the bag.

By the unmarked car Holly Blades was standing on her own. Because there was no one else to talk to, Sam crossed towards her.

"Get anything from the victim's friend?" he asked.

Holly nodded. "Ashleigh definitely left the house earlier than her mum thought – just after six. That means there was nearly an hour before she was run over."

"Right," Sam said. Holly waited for him to say more, but he

didn't. Instead he seemed distracted, as if he was thinking about something else.

"So what was that?" Holly asked, gesturing to the place where Sam had been talking to Ryan Atkins.

Sam shook his head. "Nothing," he said. "Mulvey just stopped them cos he's a twat."

Holly was surprised by the word and Sam's bitter tone. "Mulvey is?"

"Yeah."

"Why?"

Sam paused, already regretting that he'd revealed his feelings. "Doesn't matter," he said. Then he saw Sergeant Stafford emerge from the bin shelter and head their way.

"It looks like it *is* Ashleigh's bag and shoe," Stafford said when he reached them. "We'll cordon it off till Forensics arrive and then see what they can get."

"What about witnesses?" Sam asked. He gestured up at the block of flats above them. "Someone up there might have seen something."

"There'll probably be a door-to-door," Stafford said with a nod. "But not tonight. What shift are you two on tomorrow?"

"Earlies, Sarge," Holly said.

Stafford nodded. "Okay, in that case you both need to clock off. I'm heading back to the nick to give Inspector Harris an update, so you can come back with me. Fill in your day sheets but leave your individual logs till tomorrow, okay? You need to get home."

"We could stay if we're needed," Sam said.

Stafford shook his head. "You'll be more use tomorrow. Come on."

He gestured them towards his car and as Sam followed he could see Mulvey coming out of the bin shelter like it was his own personal property.

15.

SECTION HOUSE
22:04 HRS

Holly closed the front door of the Section House with her foot and went along the hall to the door of Sam's room.

"I'm back!" she called out, knocking hard on the door so she'd be heard over the music inside. "Mushy peas or beans?"

As soon as they'd changed into their civvies at the station and walked back to the house they'd tossed for who went to the chippy – Holly had lost.

In Sam's room the music dropped in volume, but only a little. "Don't care," he called back. "Gimme two minutes."

"Okay, but I'm not waiting," Holly said, moving on. She was starving.

In the kitchen she shrugged off her coat and looked for plates. Stuck to the cupboard door was a note from Yvonne in thick felt pen: *Who is cleaning bathrooms this week? Do it!!*

At one time the unattractive semi-detached house would have been occupied by a regular officer and his family, but since the introduction of the Trainee Police Officer scheme the ground floor had been converted to provide four rooms for TPOs, plus kitchen, lounge and bathrooms.

Upstairs there was a self-contained flat which was occupied

by Yvonne Dunlop, who got it at a reduced rent in exchange for being in general charge of the house – hence the message about bathroom cleaning. Yvonne was responsible for making sure the TPOs kept the place decent, didn't break the house rules and behaved responsibly. She never had much trouble doing it, either. None of the four teenagers living there wanted to cross Yvonne, on duty or off.

Holly put plates on the table and started to unwrap the food. Apart from Sam there was no one else in. The other TPOs – Tommo, who should have cleaned the bathroom, and Shiny Chris – were both on late turn at Barwick nick, and Yvonne hadn't clocked off yet. She might still be at the hospital, depending on Ashleigh Jarvis's condition. Holly would have liked to know what that was.

As she dished out the chips Sam wandered into the kitchen. His hair was wet from the shower, uncombed.

"You've got beans," Holly told him.

"Okay," he said flatly and went to the fridge in search of a drink.

Holly sat down and started on her chips. She was hungrier than she'd realised and she ate quickly before the food could get cold.

After a moment Sam sat down at the opposite side of the table. He pulled the tab on a can of Fanta and slurped it.

"Two seventy," Holly said. The cost of his pie, chips and beans.

"Okay."

"Don't forget."

"I won't."

They ate for several minutes in silence then, until finally Holly had had enough of it. Sam could be irritating when he held forth on a subject he *thought* he knew all about, but this complete silence wasn't like him. *Plus* he looked like he was brooding over something.

"Okay, so what *is* up with you?" Holly said in the end. "Something is."

Sam finished chewing his mouthful, then said: "It's just Bob Mulvey. He's a—"

"Yeah, you said that already," Holly told him. "*Why?*"

Sam shook his head.

"Okay, please yourself," Holly said. She wasn't going to play cat and mouse.

Sam picked up a chip, then changed his mind and chucked it back on his plate. "You know who found the bag and stuff in that bin shelter?" he said

The fact that he was asking the question gave Holly the answer. "You?"

"Yeah. Only Mulvey calls it in like it was him." The indignation in Sam's voice made it clear just how bitter he felt. "I wouldn't have minded if he'd said *we* found it. But he was nowhere near – he wasn't even *there*."

"You didn't tell Staff?" Holly asked.

Sam shook his head and put on a whiny little-boy voice: "*Sarge, it was me, Sarge, not him, Sarge.*"

Holly nodded. "Yeah, that wouldn't've been good." Sergeant Stafford wasn't exactly fond of people who complained. The way he saw it, *life* was unfair and if you couldn't deal with the small stuff you wouldn't be much use when the big stuff came along.

"So what are you going to do?"

"Nothing," Sam said grimly. "Except make sure that next time *I* call it in. Sod Mulvey."

He skewered a chip with his fork and bit it decisively. As he did so Holly's phone rang. She looked at the screen: *Mum*.

For a second she debated, then pressed a button. "Hi."

"Hi. It's me," her mum said.

"Hold on a sec."

Holly stood up and gestured to their plates. "Will you clear this up?"

Sam nodded. "You finished?" he asked.

"Yeah."

"Okay." He started moving the last of her chips to his own plate and Holly headed off towards her room. "Hi," she said into the phone again. "Sorry."

"It's not too late for you is it?" her mum said.

"No, it's okay. I'm on earlies tomorrow though, so I'm heading for bed in a few minutes." She let herself into her room and closed the door behind her.

"Who's there with you?"

"Just Sam." Then she added: "Yvonne's upstairs." Her mum had liked Yvonne when they met and Holly knew she worried less if she thought Yvonne was around.

"Oh. Good," her mum said.

"How's things at home?" Holly asked, sitting on the bed and unlacing her boots with one hand.

"Oh, you know – okay."

Holly paused and assessed her mother's tone, trying to work out how okay "okay" really was.

"No...*problems*?" They both knew what the euphemism referred to and although she always felt obliged to ask, it was times like this – when she was tired and just wanted to get to bed – that Holly hoped it wouldn't be the start of a much longer, more emotional conversation.

"No, no, everything's fine," her mum said. "What sort of day have you had?"

Holly relaxed a little at that and pushed her boots off. "It was all right. Nothing much. We had an RTC – Road Traffic Collision."

"Oh dear. Was anyone hurt?"

"No, it was fine," Holly said. "Nothing major."

In her head she saw the image of Ashleigh Jarvis lying in the road with no shoes on her feet, the probable victim of an accident and a rape.

"Listen," she said. "Can I call you tomorrow? I need to get to bed. Is that okay?"

"Of course, sweetie. Just as long as you're all right."

"I am," Holly said. "I'm fine."

SATURDAY

1.

MORNINGSTAR RD STATION
07:34 HRS

It was only just getting light as Holly turned the corner into Morningstar Road. She had her hands pushed deep into her coat pockets and her hat was pulled down over her ears against the icy breeze.

"Hol?"

The call came from behind her. When she turned to look she saw Sam jogging after her, his breath coming in clouds. Although he had a scarf wrapped round his neck he seemed too lightly dressed for the cold morning.

Holly waited till he was alongside her then carried on towards the station.

"Aren't you frozen?" she asked.

"Nope. Got my thermals on."

"Too much information, 'specially this early."

Sam chuckled. "Did you see Yvonne this morning?" he asked then.

"Uh-uh. Why?"

"Just wondered if they'd got any further last night – you know, on the rape case."

Holly nodded. She'd been wondering the same thing more or less from the moment she'd got out of bed.

"Suppose it'll depend if the victim came round and told them what happened," Sam went on. "We'll probably be off it anyway though. I haven't done the same thing two days running since we got here."

"No, me either," Holly said flatly.

The frontage of Morningstar Road station was red-brick Victorian, with tall windows which emitted a sickly yellow light. However, behind the original structure, a larger and more modern building had been erected on the site of demolished houses and shops. This was where the majority of the station's work was done, and there was no public access to the car park and Custody Yard which surrounded it.

At the rear gate Holly swiped her security card through the reader and when the lock clicked she held the gate open for Sam to follow. Under the gaze of several security cameras they crossed to the main building and entered the nick through heavy glass doors.

Inside it was warmer and the station corridors were getting busy with late-turn officers who'd come in to finish off reports before the end of their overnight shift. A lot of them looked tired and hassled. Unless you were on authorised overtime you wanted to get your paperwork done before the eight o'clock changeover so you could clock off on time and get home to bed.

Leaving Sam in the corridor, Holly entered the female locker room where it was quieter and smelled of an odd mixture of perfume and cleaning fluid. Her uniform and personal effects were housed in a dented metal locker near the showers and, after dialling the combination, she pulled out her gear and started to change.

On the whole there was a relaxed and fairly friendly atmosphere in the locker room, but even so, Holly still didn't feel she knew the regs well enough to enter into much of the gossip and chit-chat that went on around her. You didn't have to be in there for very long to realise that the female PCs could be every bit as raunchy and tasteless as the men, but Holly also knew that some of the women tended to moderate what they said when she was around – in particular about sex and booze. Whether that was because they were being protective or because they weren't sure how she'd take it, Holly couldn't tell.

Once she'd pulled on her uniform sweater Holly set about tying her hair back in a ponytail. As she did so she caught part of a conversation between two unseen women in a row of lockers on the far side of the room.

"So how old was she?"

"Fourteen? Something like that."

"Well, old enough round there then."

"Nah, come on..."

"No, I'm not saying she wanted it. I'm just saying if you'd got any sense you wouldn't be wandering round the Kaddy Estate on your own in the dark. I mean, that *is* asking for it. You need more sense than..."

Holly lost the rest of the conversation in the clang of a locker being closed and a sudden influx of noise from the corridor as the women went out. She finished tying her hair and closed her own locker.

Would the other PCs have thought differently if they'd seen Ashleigh Jarvis lying in the road? Probably not. Did it matter? Again, probably not. Holly knew that everyone here would tell you the same thing: don't get emotionally involved, stay objective. It was the only way to deal with the job.

She finished tying her hair and closed her own locker, quietly.

As he pushed against the door into the canteen Sam almost walked into PC Bob Mulvey.

"Whoa there, tiger!" Mulvey said like he was the first one to ever use the phrase.

"Right," Sam said. He made to move on but Mulvey continued to block the door. "Where's your girlfriend?" he asked, looking along the corridor.

Sam knew he meant Holly – yet another lame joke – but he didn't want to give Mulvey the satisfaction of acknowledging it.

"Still in bed, probably," he said.

Mulvey frowned. "She should be in by now."

"In?" Sam looked puzzled. "Why?"

"I thought she was on this morning. Sergeant Stafford reckons she is."

"Why'd he think that?" Sam said. "He doesn't know her."

"What? What're you talking about?"

"Lucy," Sam said, plucking a name from the air.

"Who the bloody hell's Lucy?" Mulvey said, his irritation showing now.

"My girlfriend," Sam said, poker-faced. "I thought you said—"

Mulvey scowled at him. "You taking the piss?"

"What? No," Sam said, feigning genuine confusion. "You said 'Where's your girlfriend?' and—"

"I meant *Holly*," Mulvey said, cutting him off.

"What's up?" Holly asked as she approached along the corridor, just in time to hear her name.

Mulvey turned quickly, as if he suspected he was the victim of an elaborate set-up, but when Holly just looked curious the PC was stymied.

"Sergeant Stafford wants you both to report to the Incident Room," he said tersely. "There's a briefing at eight."

"What sort of briefing?" Holly said.

"The Jarvis case," Mulvey said, and Sam was pleased to hear a note of resentment in his voice. "Looks like you'll be on door-to-door."

"Excellent," Sam said, and meant it.

"Don't be late," Mulvey told him and moved off. Behind his back Sam gave a broad smirk.

"What?" Holly asked.

"No, nothing," Sam said, still grinning as he watched the PC depart. "I just found out how bright Mulvey is, that's all."

2.

INCIDENT ROOM
MORNINGSTAR RD STATION
08:03 HRS

"For those of you who don't know already, the victim is Ashleigh Jane Jarvis, an IC1 female, fourteen years old."

DS Woods was standing in front of a whiteboard in the Incident Room. On a desk nearby was a laptop, which was linked up for the PowerPoint presentation. It was operated by DC Danny Simmons, a guy in his late twenties wearing a leather jacket, jeans and DMs.

When Woods nodded, Simmons tapped a key on the laptop and a school photo of Ashleigh was projected onto the whiteboard. The six uniformed officers in the room each had a copy of the same photo and, like them, Holly and Sam had their pocketbooks open, ready to make notes.

"As of 07:30 this morning Ashleigh's condition was still listed as critical but stable," Woods went on. "Which means that she's unconscious and can't tell us what happened to her. However, from the forensics we do know that she'd had intercourse recently, and because some of her clothes were found in a bin shelter on the Cadogan Estate we're taking the view that it wasn't consensual sex. We might be wrong, but we can't afford to take the chance, so we're treating this as a rape, okay?"

There were nods from the officers and Holly noticed there were none of the usual dodgy remarks that often accompanied parade briefings.

"Okay," Woods said. "Our timeline starts at 18:05 last night when Ashleigh left her friend's house saying she was going home. At 18:40 she sent a text to her mother to say she'd be home soon, and at 19:05 she was involved in the RTC on Gatemead Road. If she'd just been attacked I don't think she'd have been sending texts, so I think it's most likely that the assault took place between 18:40 and 19:05."

Danny Simmons changed the display and a map of the Cadogan Estate and surrounding streets came up on the whiteboard. Woods blew his nose into a tissue and stepped forward to indicate the locations he was talking about.

"Ashleigh's bag and clothes were found here, so that's a possible site for the attack. The RTC happened here – a distance of about three hundred metres. Now, the bin shelter isn't on a direct route through the estate, so there's a possibility that Ashleigh was taken there by force, or alternatively that she was led there by someone she knew. Whichever it was, we need to know if anyone saw her – either alone or with someone else – in this area between 18:00 and 19:00 hours.

"We'll be doing a door-to-door on the properties along her probable route and we'll also be manning the cordon round the bin shelter and talking to anyone who passes it. Did they see her? Was there anyone acting suspiciously in the area – running away, sitting in a vehicle, kerb crawling…?"

From the front row of chairs, Oz Sitwell looked up from his notes. "Are we going to get DNA from the rape kit?"

Woods nodded. "It looks likely. There was semen present, so either he's stupid or he doesn't care."

Another reg spoke up from the side. "Have we got any known paedos in the area, Sarge? I'm thinking about her age. Could she have been a target because she was young?"

Woods reached for another tissue and nodded. "We're checking known sexual offenders on the Register, but at the moment nothing's come up. Age could be a factor, but for the time being I want to keep an open mind."

He sniffed, rubbed his nose and looked round. "Any other questions?"

There weren't.

"Right. As far as members of the public are concerned, remember it's the Cadogan, so half the estate probably know what went on – or think they do. Even so, the line is that we're investigating a serious assault and beyond that, no specifics. For the moment I want to keep the rape aspect to ourselves."

He glanced down at a piece of paper. "Okay – assignments: PC Ellis, PC Lester and TPO Blades are with Danny on the cordon, everyone else on the door-to-door. We're on channel three for radios and there'll be a van at the scene, so that's our command point. We'll leave in five from the yard."

He blew his nose noisily and at that signal there was a scraping of chairs and a rise in the chatter as the assembled officers got to their feet. As Sam and Holly put their pocketbooks away Oz Sitwell came over.

"Sam, you're with me on door-to-door. Grab your jacket, you'll need it."

"Right." Sam moved off, looking pleased.

"You too, Hol," Oz said.

Holly nodded but gestured to the room, uncertain. "Who am I paired with?"

"No one. You're OR."

OR stood for *Own Recognisance* and it meant she'd be working without the direct supervision of a training officer. So far this had only happened when she'd been assigned to tasks inside the station – things that didn't have implications for a serious ongoing enquiry.

"Are you sure?" Holly asked.

Oz nodded. "No one available. You'll be okay though. Cordon duty's just standing around. Someone comes up to you, ask them if they were in the area last night and whether they saw anything. If they did and it sounds useful, get their name and contact details down on a WS2 form and call Danny Simmons or DS Woods. If it's just a local being nosey, send them away, okay?"

"Okay," Holly said, still a little uncertain.

Oz nodded. "The only thing you'll really have to worry about is keeping warm and not being able to go for a pee."

3

From his vantage point on the sixth-floor balcony Drew Alford could see the fluttering blue and white tape that cordoned off the service road and all access to it. He could see the coppers standing nearby, questioning anyone who approached, and he could see the forensic-suited people coming and going from the bin shelter.

Some time in the night a large plastic tent had been erected over the shelter, blocking the view of the inside, but seeing what was going on around it was enough. Alford had watched plenty of news stories and TV series and he knew that the forensics people would be trying to find DNA and other traces of anyone who had been near the bins last night.

That was what puzzled him, though. He'd known there might be police around today, asking questions, but what he couldn't work out was *why* they were doing all the rest. It wasn't like there'd been a murder or something, so why all the effort?

Below him, some uniform coppers gathered together in a group by their van. A plain-clothed guy was talking to them. He gestured towards the cordon and then towards the block of flats, and when he did so Alford instinctively took a step back from the balcony rail. Time to move on. He was getting cold anyway.

He turned towards the stairwell and saw Skank coming out of the entrance.

"Oi-oi," Skank said in greeting. "You seen what's happening down there?"

"I've seen it. What's it for?"

"My old man says it was a rape," Skank said, moving to the railing to look down at the view.

Drew Alford looked at him sharply. "How'd he know that?"

"I dunno, do I? He said that's what they reckoned in The Compass last night. It's a girl from school an' all. She gets raped, and then runs into the road an' gets knocked over. Ashleigh something. Jarvis. You know her?"

"No," Alford said.

"You want to go down and look?"

"No."

"Okay," Skank said, as if he didn't care one way or the other.

Alford took a moment, looking down at the activity below. His eyes were narrowed in thought.

"So what we doing?" Skank asked.

Alford refocused his attention. "Dunno yet," he said.

He started towards the stairs and Skank fell in beside him, then gave a low whistle when he saw a girl approaching along the adjoining landing. She was a bit younger than Alford and Skank with dark hair and skinny jeans. And although she knew both boys were watching her, she gave no sign until she was less than a couple of paces away.

"All right, Taz," Skank said, making no secret of his appreciative leer. "Where you going?"

"Anywhere you're not," Taz said.

Out of nowhere, Skank suddenly clutched his heart and pretended to be mortally injured. "Oh! Oh! Please!" he cried out.

"Fuck off," Alford told him, irritated. He turned to Taz. "You gonna see Bex?"

"Yeah, maybe," Taz said.

"Okay. Tell her I'll see her down the precinct later. I got something to do first."

"Why don't you call her? You were *supposed* to see her last night."

"Yeah, well, I had something else on," Alford said brusquely.

Skank sniggered knowingly until Alford gave him a black look.

"Just tell her, all right," he said, turning his attention back to Taz. "'Bout an hour."

Taz held his gaze for a second, then nodded. When she looked away Skank took the opportunity to engage her again.

"You know Ashleigh Jarvis, right?" he asked.

"What about her?" Taz said, reluctant to encourage him but curious, too.

"Didn't you see what's going on down there?" Skank gestured over the railing. "She's in hospital – Ash – in a coma. They reckon she was raped last night, then got run over."

"Who you working for, *The Six O'Clock News*?" Alford said acidly. "Don't forget to tell Bex," he said to Taz, then pushed Skank towards the stairwell.

As Taz moved away along the landing Skank glanced back at her, enjoying the sight of her tight jeans.

"I could give her one," he said, as if he'd given the matter a lot of thought. "Taz, I mean," he added quickly, so Alford wouldn't think he was talking about Bex.

"You'd be fuckin' lucky," Alford said. "She hates you."

"Doesn't mean I wouldn't though," Skank said ruefully.

"Yeah it does," Alford said flatly. "No chance."

4.

SCENE OF CRIME
CADOGAN ESTATE
09:35 HRS

From the edge of the outer cordon Holly watched as a female Crime Scene Examiner carried a handful of sealed evidence bags out of the forensic tent and across to a van. Except for her face every part of her was covered by a white forensic suit. Her hands were gloved and her boots were invisible beneath blue plastic overshoes.

For the first half-hour Holly had been stationed at the inner cordon with the job of lifting the tape as the CSEs went in and out of the bin shelter with equipment or evidence bags. From there she'd been close enough to catch the occasional glimpse of what they were doing inside: dusting the galvanised bins for prints, taking sample swabs from bags and cardboard.

Watching this had been enough to stave off the boredom of the job, but then DC Simmons had asked her to relocate to the outer cordon and keep an eye on the forensic team's van. From then on the only thing to distract her was the cold in her feet and the occasional curious passer-by.

When anyone did approach, Holly asked the same question: "*Were you near here between six and seven o'clock yesterday evening?*" And when they said no – as they invariably did – she asked them to move on as politely as possible.

Now Holly watched as the female CSE put the evidence bags in the van and locked it. From the size and shape of the bags, she was pretty sure they contained Ashleigh Jarvis's coat, bag and shoes, so when the CSE glanced her way and gave a friendly nod Holly took the opportunity to speak.

"How's it going?" she asked.

"We've had worse," the CSE said. She hesitated, then came a bit closer. "First serious crime scene?"

Holly nodded. "We were here last night. One of the other TPOs found the victim's things."

"Yeah? They did well to spot them in there."

"Do you think you'll be able to get any evidence to show who did it?"

The CSE pulled a face. "Maybe. Problem is, it's a communal area, so most of the samples we get will be unrelated." She gestured towards the bin shelter. "If we find a fag end on the victim's coat, we could get DNA from it, but we still wouldn't know whether it came from the attacker or Mrs Bloggin's rubbish."

"So it's a waste of time?"

"No, but I reckon the best chance of a result will be from the rape kit, the knickers or the rest of her clothes. If we get a foreign DNA sample there that's going to be the best pointer towards the culprit."

"*If* he's on file."

"Yeah, well, if they'd let us have everyone's DNA on record… Course, civil liberties would have something to say about that."

She shrugged, then shifted. "Listen, I'd better get on."

"Sure. Thanks." Holly hunched against a gust of cold wind. "How much longer will it take do you know?"

"Couple of hours probably. Sorry."

"Nah, I'll survive," Holly said.

5.

DRURY HOUSE
CADOGAN ESTATE
09:38 HRS

"Okay, thanks for your help."

Oz Sitwell stepped back and made a note on his clipboard as the woman inside the flat closed the door. They were on the eighth-floor landing of Drury House because Oz reckoned it was easier to start at the top and work down.

"Five for seven," Oz said, meaning five answers from seven doors. "Not bad for a Saturday morning so far."

"So what happens for the places where no one's in?" Sam asked. "I mean, when do we try again?"

"That's up to CID. If they think it's worth spending their budget we can keep on coming back till we've talked to everyone in the block. Don't think they'll do it on this though, not unless she dies. If she does the budget'll go up."

He gestured towards the next door and Sam moved with him.

"The thing I don't get is why we need to do door-to-door in the first place," Sam said. "I mean, if someone knows something or saw something, aren't they going to come forward and say?"

"You'd think, but they don't," Oz said, with a flat shrug. "They can't be arsed."

"What, even for something serious like this?"

"Not serious to them, is it?"

He took hold of the letter box flap in the next door and rattled it sharply.

"Couple of years back we did a door-to-door for a stabbing in Covington. The DI's convinced there must've been witnesses so we went all round the streets about five times; kept going back till we'd talked to all the residents except one... Finally we go round and find this bloke at home and as soon as we tell him what it's about he says, 'Oh, yeah, I knew you'd been round. I saw the bloke you want: big white guy with a beard. He chucked the knife in a hedge.' We ask him to show us the hedge and there's the knife – fingerprints, DNA, the lot."

"So why didn't he come forward or call in?"

"That's what we asked him, and he says, 'That's *your* job, innit – to come to me.' Real public spirit."

There was no answer at the door and Oz wrote *NA* against the number of the flat on his sheet, then looked at Sam. "Okay, let's speed this up. You take the next one. I'll go and start in from the other end. After that we'll take different floors. Reckon you can handle that?"

"Sure," Sam said. It didn't seem like rocket science.

"Right," Oz said. He handed Sam the clipboard, then headed off towards the far end of the walkway.

6

The car's engine ticked over and the heater blew warm air from the footwell laced with Tommy Vickers's eau de cologne. In the passenger seat behind the tinted glass windows, Drew Alford watched as Vickers peeled five twenty-pound notes off a roll he'd taken from his jacket pocket. The roll was too big to encompass with one hand – even Vickers's hand, which was large and beefy like the man – and the hundred quid being removed made no appreciable difference to its size.

Vickers offered the notes, but withheld them for a moment when Alford made to take them.

"If anyone says it was you, you're gonna take it on your own, right?"

Alford nodded. "There was only the owner and his missis and they didn't see who we were."

"Okay then."

Vickers tipped the notes forwards again and this time let Alford take them. "Don't go near the place again – not unless I say."

"Sure, no problem," Alford said. Then: "So, did you collect? – From the shop, I mean?"

Vickers eyed him coolly for a moment, then half nodded. "It'll be sorted," he said.

"Right," Alford said. "So is there anything else you want me to do?"

"I'll let you know. There could be something. Maybe." Then he changed the subject with a tilt of his head. "You know anything about that girl on the estate last night?"

Alford shook his head. "We was doing the shop when it happened. First I knew was seeing the coppers all over the place this morning."

"Right. Best keep your head down then – till they clear out. I'll be in touch, all right?"

"Okay," Alford said, knowing he'd been dismissed. "I'll see you later. Thanks."

And with that he reached for the door handle.

As Tommy Vickers's Merc pulled away, Drew Alford fingered the notes in his pocket and did some maths. He'd originally thought of giving twenty quid each to Skank, Tyler and Rizza, leaving himself with forty. But now that he had the money, he couldn't see any reason not to make it a sixty-forty split – after all, the others wouldn't have got anything without him setting it up.

Nah, sod it, he decided, they could fight it out between themselves how they split forty quid three ways. They were lucky to be getting that.

7.

SCENE OF CRIME
CADOGAN ESTATE
10:40 HRS

"D'you know what happened then?"

Holly had watched the girl approaching, checking out the lie of the land, chewing gum. She was quite open about her curiosity, as if she had every right to look.

"There was a serious incident here last night," Holly said – the standard reply.

"Yeah, I know *that*," the girl said, snapping her gum. "I mean, you know who *done* it?"

"We're still making enquiries," Holly said.

"So you don't."

Holly looked the girl over. At a guess she was about fourteen, though she could probably pass for older if she tried. She was quite pretty, with long, dark hair – darker than natural – and just a bit too much eyeliner. Her clothes were from the cheap end of Topshop or the top end of Primark.

"Were you anywhere near here yesterday evening?" Holly asked. "Between six and seven?"

"Me? Nah." The girl shook her head. "I just heard it was Ash – Ashleigh, right?"

"That's right. Do you know her?"

"A bit. We're not best mates nor nothin'. Same school, that's all."

Holly nodded. "What's your name?"

The girl hesitated for a beat, then said, "Taz."

"Taz?"

"Tamsin. Stupid, innit?"

"I don't know," Holly said. "It's unusual. I've never heard of anyone else called that."

"No, cos no one else'd give such a crap name to a kid – no one 'cept my mum anyway."

"Do you live around here?" Holly asked, gesturing towards the blocks of flats.

"Not here: Penrice House. It's just as bad as this though."

Holly didn't make any comment on that. Instead she said: "Does Ashleigh know anyone else on the estate? We're just trying to work out who she might have seen before she was hurt."

Taz gave her a knowing look. "You don't mean hurt by the lorry, right? People say she was raped. That true?"

"We don't know yet," Holly said, choosing her words carefully. "We're still making enquiries. Can you tell me anything about Ashleigh's friends – who she might've seen?"

She expected the girl to just say "no" and clam up like everyone else had done, but instead Taz made an odd kind of shuffle, as if she was trying to make up her mind about something. Then she cast a look around.

"Listen, I'm not saying nothing here, okay? People see me..." She pulled a face.

Holly took a moment, then pressed the girl. "Ashleigh was hurt pretty badly," she said. "If you know her and you could help us find out who did it you'd really be helping. No one else needs to know."

Taz hesitated, then she said, "What's your name?"

"Holly. Holly Blades."

"Okay. I might go down the market later – Crisp Street, yeah? Might be in the caff. 'Bout an hour – just you, though."

"Listen—" Holly began.

But Taz was already turning away and moving back the way she'd come. "I live here," she was saying irritatedly and loud enough for anyone nearby to hear. "I got a *right* to go through. Stupid plods!"

And it was that – the smart way Taz had covered herself – that made up Holly's mind. She reached for her radio.

"DC Simmons from Seven-Six-Two, receiving?"

A few metres away Taz rounded a corner and disappeared from sight without a backwards look.

"*Go ahead,*" Simmons said over the radio earpiece.

"It's TPO Blades on the cordon. Could I talk to you for a minute?"

8.

CRISP STREET MARKET
11:34 HRS

As the car pulled in at the kerb Holly knew that DC Simmons wasn't fully convinced by all this, and now neither was she. Or at least, she was less convinced than she had been before.

To begin with she'd been pretty sure that Taz knew something about last night and was willing to talk about it. But the more Simmons and DS Woods had discussed it – along with the practicalities of a meeting – the more Holly had started to realise that she'd gone out on a limb. If Taz *had* just been spinning her a line and didn't turn up, this was going to be seen as a massive waste of time: her fault.

But, for good or bad, they were here now and instead of her uniform jacket and vest, Holly was wearing a dark grey fleece several sizes too large for her. It had a lingering scent of Danny Simmons's aftershave – not unpleasant, but definitely not Estée Lauder.

Simmons switched off the engine and turned to face her. He had a day's worth of stubble on his chin. "Scruffy", her mum would call him, although he was good-looking enough.

"Okay, so you know how this works?" Simmons asked, his expression serious.

Holly nodded. "I think so."

"Tell me again."

"I'm not allowed to offer any inducements for information and I can't say anything about the rape. All I can tell her is that Ashleigh was attacked some time before she was knocked over."

"Right," Danny Simmons said. "You also need to find out her full name, an address if possible, and some way to contact her. It's no good if she tells you something useful and then we can't get hold of her again."

Holly nodded. "What if she says she knows something but won't tell me unless I offer her money?"

"Best you can do is say you'll have to talk to someone senior, then make an arrangement to meet her again. But if she's only there because she thinks she can make a few quid she's probably going to be unreliable anyway."

He looked at Holly, weighing her up, then seemed to thaw a little. "DS Woods says you're smart," he said. "So just see what you can pick up, okay? Remember, the best way to get someone to talk to you is to keep quiet. People don't like silences. They want to fill them, so they tell you things."

"Okay," Holly said. She was a bit thrown by the apparent compliment DS Woods had paid her.

"You got any money?"

"Er, yeah, a bit."

Simmons dug in his pocket and took out his wallet. He gave her a fiver. "Take that. Buy her a drink, and yourself." He looked at his watch. "If she's not there already we'll give her half an hour."

"Where will you be?"

"Getting cold. Ready?"

"Yeah."

"Okay then." And he turned to open his door.

9

Drew Alford had his arm round Bex's shoulders, drawing her closer so he could whisper in her ear. His other hand was inside her coat, out of sight. Bex listened to him for a moment, then giggled and hit his arm as if scandalised by what he'd said. She didn't pull away though.

Leaning on the railings, Taz watched the two of them, bored. She pushed her hands deeper in her pockets and chewed her gum, ignoring Skank as best she could.

She'd tried to persuade Bex not to go to the precinct. It would pay Drew back for standing Bex up last night, Taz told her friend: serve him right. Anyway, the precinct was boring and there was nothing to do: they should go somewhere else, sod Drew.

But Bex didn't have any money and she thought she could get Drew to buy her something to make up for not showing last night, so in the end they went to the precinct and hung around till Drew finally loped into sight with Skank.

If she could have left then, Taz would have. Drew had this way of looking at you like he could tell what you were thinking, and after talking to the girl copper outside the flats Taz was even less comfortable being near him. As it turned out, though, she needn't have worried about Drew's intuition. When he walked up he barely acknowledged her

– instead offering a half-hearted apology to Bex for not showing last night. And when Bex finally let him off he put a possessive arm round her waist and slipped his hand into the back pocket of her jeans. The two of them stayed like that – walking like they were welded at the hip – while they all did a circuit of the shops and finally came to a halt at their usual bench in the square.

So now, after ten minutes of watching Bex and Drew snog and giggle and moving away every time Skank edged closer, Taz was restless, wanting to get away. At some point soon she knew Drew would decide he'd gone as far as he could with Bex in public and he'd want to go off somewhere more private – probably his place. That would leave Taz alone with Skank, who was harder to shake off than warts, so she knew she'd better make her move now.

"Listen, I'm gonna go, okay?" she said to Bex and pushed herself away from the railings. "I told my mum I'd be back. I'll see you later, yeah?"

Bex disengaged herself a little from Drew's arm. "Hang on. You don't have to go," she said. "We can all do something."

Drew leaned in again and whispered in her ear, and this time Bex hit him for real. "Get out!" she said. "No way!"

Drew shrugged. "Just asking," he said.

"It's okay," Taz said, already moving. "I'll see you later. Give me a ring, yeah?"

"Okay."

"Hang on," Skank said, moving to cut in front of Taz. "Madder's got some puff. If you want we could find him. You and me, I mean."

Taz stepped aside, not bothering to hide the fact that Skank was the last person on earth she'd go anywhere with. "Get lost, Skank," she said flatly. And with that she was away.

Drew Alford watched her go for a moment, then looked at Skank. "Told you," he said, a malicious grin on his face.

"Told him what?" Bex asked.

"Nothing – so, we going to mine or what?"

"You sure she's out?"

"Yeah, I told you."

Bex shrugged. "Okay then," she said. "Can we go to Boots on the way? I need some nail polish."

Alford shrugged, then grinned. "Better get a pack of three an' all."

"You want me to come, too?" Skank asked as Alford stood up, pulling Bex with him.

"What for?"

"I dunno, I just thought..."

"Thought wrong then," Alford said. "Go and find Tyler and Riz – give 'em their cut."

"What cut?" Bex asked.

"Nothing," Alford said, and to Skank: "Well go on then. Jesus!"

10.

PANTRY CAFE
CRISP STREET MARKET
12:02 HRS

There were a few other people in the cafe, one or two on their own, but most with someone else, chatting over food or drinks. The large plate-glass windows were thick with condensation and decorated with handwritten signs on luminous card: Breakfast special £2.99; Sandwiches Freshly Made and a dozen more like it. Holly had read each one several times over as she nursed the last cold inch of coffee in her mug. It was nearly half an hour since she'd sat down and by now she was pretty certain that Taz wasn't going to show.

She looked at her watch for the twentieth time and then the door opened and she saw Taz enter quickly, furtively, and look round. When she spotted Holly she hesitated for a second, as if she didn't quite recognize her without her uniform. Holly raised a hand in greeting though, and Taz came over to the table and sat down, her back to the door.

"Hiya," Holly said brightly, as much with relief as anything. "Thanks for coming. Can I get you a drink or something?"

Taz nodded. "Coke," she said.

"Okay, hold on."

At the counter Holly bought another coffee, a can of Coke and two iced fingers from a display case. She carried them back to the table on a tray and sat down again. "I thought you might want something to eat. You like iced fingers?"

"They're all right," Taz said, snapping her gum.

"I love them," Holly said. "Go on, you'd better eat one or I won't be able to stop myself having both."

For a moment Taz seemed to think about it, then she took out her gum, stuck it under the table and picked up an iced finger. Holly waited till she took a bite, then sipped her coffee.

"So what did you want to tell me?" she asked.

She hoped she was tackling this right – just coming out and asking the question – but there didn't seem any point in pretending that wasn't why they were here.

Taz chewed her bun for a moment or two longer, then said: "I don't know who did it, right? I wasn't there."

"Okay," Holly said, giving it time.

Taz nodded, as if she'd needed to make that clear before they went on. Then she pulled the ring on the can of Coke. "How long you been a copper?" she asked. "How old are you?"

"I'm a TPO – a trainee," Holly said. "It's my first year."

"So – how old?"

"Sixteen and a half."

Taz snorted. "You sound like my little brother. Ask him and he says he's seven years and five months and three days."

"What about you?" Holly said, wanting to turn the conversation back on to Taz.

"Guess."

Holly pursed her lips and pretended to assess her. "Fifteen," she lied.

"Near enough," Taz said, but she seemed pleased. She hesitated for a second longer. "No one's gonna know I was here, yeah? Cos I wasn't – right?"

"No, it's just between us," Holly said. Then she waited, remembering what Danny Simmons had said about silence.

For a moment Taz didn't say anything. She put her hand on the Coke can and began turning it, a fraction at a time, as if she was turning back a clock.

She said: "Me and Ash, we used to be mates. I mean, better mates than we are now."

"You fell out?"

"Nah, not really. It was— I just started hanging out with Bex more. Bex don't really like Ash cos she's a bit – I dunno – a bit *young*. You know what I mean?"

Holly nodded. "So what can you tell me about yesterday?"

Taz pursed her lips. "Okay, listen," she said. "All I know, right, is you wanna talk to Drew – Drew Alford."

After she'd said his name she glanced round, as if to make sure no one had heard her.

"Why?" Holly said. "I mean, why do you think he might have something to do with what happened to Ashleigh?"

"I'm not saying he did, right? I'm just saying he could've. He could've thought Ash'd said something – you know, dissed him."

"Did she?"

Taz shifted in her seat. "Listen," she said. "Drew's going out with Bex, right? Least he's supposed to be. So yesterday lunch I'm with Bex and we're talking about Drew, right? I mean, Bex was. She was saying how he was messing her about, not calling her when he said he would, stuff like that. So I said maybe she should dump him."

She looked at Holly. "I was only saying it cos Bex was being all down on him, right? But as soon as I said it she's all, 'Why're you saying that? Is it cos *you* want to get off with him?' And I'm, like, '*No!*' But she's getting all worked up, so in the end... In the end I said it's not me she needs to worry about. And she says, 'What's that mean?' And that's when I tell her how I've heard Drew telling Tyler about how he fancies Ash."

She looked down at the Coke can and Holly recognised that this was important. Taz was feeling guilty.

"I didn't– It didn't mean anything," Taz said. "I mean, I didn't know Bex was gonna have a go at Ash about it – I just thought she'd see what Drew was really like – you know, fancying other girls on the side."

She broke off, frowned for a moment, like it was a bad memory.

"Thing is," she went on, "Bex doesn't see it like that. She thinks it's Ash's fault, so she says she's gonna have it out with her – you know, '*Are you trying to nick my bloke?*' – right? – so when we see Ash later, Bex is straight in and Ash is all 'No. No way.' – but Bex won't believe it, she won't stop going on, so in the end Ash says she wouldn't *want* to get off with Drew cos he's a tosser and she reckons you'd probably catch something like herpes or Aids."

"What did Bex say to that?" Holly asked, although she could already guess at the answer.

Taz made a snort, as if it was a stupid question. "She says, '*Don't you dis Drew. You're gonna be in trouble saying stuff like that about him.*' – And it's true, right? That's what I'm saying – if Drew knew Ash'd said stuff like that about him he's not gonna let it go, is he? '*Specially* not Drew."

"Why 'specially?" Holly asked.

Taz scowled scornfully. "Cos he thinks he's cock of the walk. Cos he thinks it's okay for him to call any girl a slag or whatever, but he ain't gonna put up with it back. No way."

Holly took a moment, running back over the whole thing. As a motive for rape an insult seemed a bit thin, but from Taz's expression it was clear she was taking this pretty seriously.

"Was it true?" Holly asked then. "*Does* Drew fancy Ashleigh?"

Taz nodded. "I heard him and some of the other lads talking about her a few weeks ago. Drew said she was a nine – you know, out of ten? He's always saying stuff like 'She's a three, she's an eight'. He doesn't care if you hear it or not. That's what they're like. I told you before though – you answer them back, you stick up for yourself and that's disrespect, innit?"

"So you think Drew might have known what Ashleigh said about him?"

"I don't think – I *know*," Taz said.

"How?"

"Cos I saw him with her yesterday afternoon."

"With Ashleigh?"

Taz nodded. "On the estate, after school. I was going home. Ash was with another girl – I don't know her; she's from school though. It looked like Drew had stopped them. He was pointing his finger at them, saying something. I could tell he was mad."

"You mean he was threatening them?"

"Yeah, that's what it looked like."

"Then what happened?"

"Nothing. I mean, Drew's with them, then he lets them walk off."

Holly thought for a moment. She believed what Taz had told her, but she wasn't sure Danny Simmons or DS Woods would be convinced. The ups and downs and falling-outs of teenage friendships would be a closed book to them – a different world.

"Taz, listen," she said. "I think you should tell one of the CID officers what you've told me. If you—"

But Taz was already shaking her head. "No way," she said. "I'm not making a statement or nothing. If Drew finds out— I'm just not."

"No one else will know," Holly said, even though she wasn't sure that was true. "Just talk to them."

"No, I gotta go," Taz said, her mind made up now. She pushed her chair back, stood up.

"Okay, listen, just give me your phone number then. I won't give it to anyone else. I promise."

Taz hesitated, then started to rattle off a number.

"Hold on." Holly grabbed a napkin and pen and when Taz repeated the number she scribbled it down.

"I'll call you later," Holly said. "Just think about it – talking to CID."

"I told you everything," Taz said. "I've gotta go."

And with that she moved round the table and headed quickly away across the cafe.

Holly let out a sigh of resignation and watched until the cafe door closed behind Taz, then she folded the napkin and put it into her pocket. She left the iced bun on her plate, untouched.

11

For a moment Tyler Smith took his attention away from watching the open approach to Cloudsley House and looked at the notes Skank was holding.

"How much?" he asked.

"Forty."

"Okay." Tyler held out his hand for the cash.

"No, not each. That's between you, me an' Riz. Three ways."

Tyler frowned. "So how much is that?"

"Thirteen and a bit."

"That all?" Tyler sounded disbelieving.

"Ask Drew, you don't believe me."

Tyler thought about it, then dismissed the idea. He gestured for the cash again.

"I'll have to get it changed," Skank said. "This is two twenties."

"Gimme one then, I'll change it."

"Nah, it's okay, I'll do it."

"Give," Tyler said.

Reluctantly Skank handed over one of the notes, knowing he and Riz had just lost out and had no chance of getting their full whack now.

"So what you gonna do?" Skank asked as Tyler pushed

the twenty into his pocket.

"'Bout what?" Tyler gave him a sharp look. "What you talking about?"

"Nothing. I mean what you gonna do *now*? – We could find Riz, then go round to Madder's an' get some puff."

"Oh," Tyler said. Then he shook his head. "Nah. You go. I might come later." He didn't want to start smoking until he'd found Choirboy and made sure the kid knew what would happen if he said anything about last night.

"Why? Where you going?" Skank asked.

"Nowhere," Tyler said, making it clear that was all he was going to say on the matter. Then a thought: "Where's Drew?"

"Gone round to his with Bex – shagging."

"Right."

Tyler looked away to check out the people crossing the cracked paving stones and dodging the puddles. That was when he saw Choirboy coming from the direction of the precinct with a carrier bag in his hand.

"You sure you don't want to come to Madder's?" Skank asked again. He was still thinking about the twenty and ways he could get Tyler to spend some of it.

"No, I told you. Now fuck off, all right?"

Skank gave it up.

"I'll see you later then," he said.

Skank moved off, heading towards Madder's block, and Tyler watched just long enough to be sure he was gone before switching his attention back to Charlie Atkins. The boy was approaching the stairwell of Cloudsley House now, and before he could disappear from sight, Tyler set off after him at a jog.

12.

INCIDENT ROOM
MORNINGSTAR RD STATION
13:11 HRS

Standing beside the whiteboards in the Incident Room, Holly wondered if she might have been forgotten. At the far end of the room DS Woods and Danny Simmons were talking together, while the other officers – CID and uniform – went about the business of the case; manning phones and computers and collating information.

Holly wasn't involved in any of that, which left her feeling like a spare part. Rather than just stand there looking useless, she focused on the whiteboards and examined the known facts of the case, studying the various names, times and locations written up in blue marker pen.

New photographs had been added since this morning, most taken inside the bin shelter. They showed crumpled pink knickers on damp concrete, a discarded coat and a partially hidden sequined bag. And it was these Holly found most disturbing – not because of what they showed, but because of what they didn't.

All these items belonged to Ashleigh Jarvis – they were personal, private or intimate to her. But in the clinical photographs they looked starkly *impersonal*. Put on display like that they weren't belongings, just objects to be scrutinised, tested and talked about as potential evidence to what had really happened to Ashleigh last night.

While Holly was still studying the pictures, DS Woods came up beside her. In the background Danny Simmons had moved to a computer terminal.

"Tell me what happened with this girl, Taz," Woods said. "What was her reason for putting Drew Alford in the frame?"

"She reckoned Ashleigh had said things about Alford to his girlfriend, Bex: she'd disrespected him."

At the word "disrespect" Woods made a contemptuous noise. "So it's all teenage girl stuff then – who fancies who, who's friends and who's not?"

"Pretty much, yes, Sarge."

"What about Taz? Do you think she's reliable or could she have some reason to try and drop Alford in it?"

"No, I don't think so. I think she feels guilty that she might have stirred it all up."

"Right," Woods said without showing whether he was convinced or not. He dug in his pocket for a tissue and blew his nose. As he did so Danny Simmons came over, several sheets of paper in his hand.

"Drew Alford's on record," he said to Woods. "Age fifteen, lives in Penrice House. Couple of cautions for antisocial behaviour and a charge of robbery from November. That's still waiting for a court date. Intel has him down as a member of the

Kaddy Boys gang on the estate, probably the leader. Long list of associates, most of them about the same age or a bit younger."

"What's the story on the robbery charge?" Woods asked.

Simmons consulted a couple of printouts in his hand. "Looks like a mugging. Three youths took a woman's mobile and purse on Tansley Road. Alford was stopped half an hour later and he had her credit cards."

"Any violence?"

"The victim wasn't hurt but she was pushed into a doorway and threatened. Alford went no comment in interview, wouldn't say who was with him."

"Proper little pro – anyone mentioned his name on the door-to-door?"

"Not so far." Simmons leafed through some more sheets of paper. "A couple of people say they saw two or three youths in the general area at *around* the time we're looking at, but they're vague. At a push one of the descriptions *might* match Alford, but it's nothing I'd want to put in front of the CPS."

"Right."

"You think he's worth a tug?" Simmons asked. "Ashleigh slags him off so he rapes her as a punishment…?"

Woods looked dubious. "I'd want to know for certain that he did threaten Ashleigh first."

"Lauren Booth could confirm that," Holly said. "Taz said that Ashleigh was with another girl from school when Alford threatened her. If the other girl was Lauren, it could explain why she didn't want Ashleigh to walk home alone last night."

Woods sucked his throat sweet for a moment, then crunched it between his teeth.

"I suppose we'd better go and see if Lauren's at home then," he said. "You didn't have anything better to do with your Saturday afternoon, did you?"

13

In the stairwell Charlie's footsteps echoed back at him as he tried to take the steps two at a time. It was hard though, with the weight of the groceries throwing him off balance and the rising panic of knowing he wasn't going to escape.

Behind him Tyler Smith was pulling himself upwards with the aid of the handrail, closing the gap until finally he judged himself close enough and made a lunge.

He caught hold of Charlie's calf, felt his grip slide for a moment, then tighten round the boy's ankle. Charlie yelled as he fell, brought down part way onto the landing. The carrier bag slipped from his hand and spilled its contents in a clatter of tins and the flurry of a newspaper falling apart.

For a moment they were tangled together, Tyler still grasping Charlie's ankle, but when Charlie started to kick against him Tyler reached up and punched him hard in the leg.

Charlie let out a cry of pain and when Tyler finally let go of his ankle he scuttled back into the corner of the landing. Tyler pushed himself to his feet, then moved in quickly to bend over Charlie and hit him again, in the face this time, catching him on the corner of the mouth.

"Don't fucking run away from me," he said viciously. "You stop when I tell you."

14.

CLOUDSLEY HOUSE
CADOGAN ESTATE
13:15 HRS

There was only the ground floor left to do, and as Sam entered the stairs and started downwards his attention was more on his clipboard list than anything else. As a result, when he saw the figure on the stairs below it took him a moment to register that something was going on.

The boy was fourteen, maybe fifteen, stockily built with cropped blond hair. He was standing over a smaller black kid and his fist was cocked back, threatening, as the younger boy cowered in the corner of the landing.

"Oi! Hold it!" Sam shouted. "Stop there."

Sam didn't know where either the words or the commanding tone had come from, but as soon as the blond boy heard them he looked up with a defiant glare and a scowl of annoyance.

Sam took two more steps downwards, then paused at the turn of the handrail. He could see the older boy registering his uniform and for a moment neither one of them moved.

"Stand back from him," Sam said, glad it came out as confidently as before. "What's going on?"

"Mind your own business."

The blond boy's scowl had changed to a sneer and Sam knew he was weighing him up. His balled fist didn't relax.

"Are you okay?" Sam said to the kid in the corner. The boy didn't look okay but he said nothing, and Sam didn't want to take his eye off the bigger lad to assess him more closely.

"He's all right," the blond youth said. There was a growing note of defiance in his voice, refusing to give way.

Sam knew he had to take control of the situation or lose it entirely so he stiffened himself.

"I said, stand back from him," he said. "Then I want your name and address."

"I ain't telling you nothing – 'less you think you can *make* me." And he brought up his other fist, showing himself ready.

For a second Sam's right hand moved instinctively towards the baton on his belt, but he knew that a fight wouldn't help anything, so instead he reached for his radio.

"Three-One-Seven from Six-One-Four, assistance required. Stairwell, south end of the block."

It was enough. With a sneer the blond youth said, "Fuck off," then swung himself round and started down the stairs two or three at a time.

"*On way,*" Oz said over the radio. "*What's your situation?*"

"IC1 male teenager heading down the stairs. Blond. Grey jacket. Possible assault."

Sam moved to look over the handrail and down, but even though he could still hear trainers slapping on the stairs below he couldn't see anything. He knew there was no chance of catching the suspect now, so he turned back to the kid in the corner.

"You okay?" he asked.

The kid nodded, and after a moment he pushed himself up off the floor.

"What's your name?"

"Charlie," the boy said and winced. He raised a hand to examine the cut at the edge of his mouth.

Sam looked at him again, more closely. "Didn't I talk to you last night, with a couple of other lads? Charlie Atkins?"

Charlie nodded.

"So who was that? Do you know him?"

The boy called Charlie hesitated for a beat, then shook his head.

"So what happened?"

"Nothing," Charlie said. "It's okay. I just need to get my stuff."

He moved to retrieve a tin of baked beans from the step below him as Oz's voice came through on the radio.

"*Six-One-Four from Three-One-Seven. No sign of your suspect. Where are you now?*"

"Still on the stairs. Second floor."

"*Okay, stay there. I'll find you.*"

"Received." Sam turned back to Charlie. "If you know who he was, you can tell me," he said.

Charlie shook his head, more definite now. "I don't," he said.

15.

ATKINS FLAT
CLOUDSLEY HOUSE
13:19 HRS

"You know who it was? Then tell the officers."

Leyton Atkins was a man in his forties, hair greying at the sides. He wore a collar and tie and had a pair of reading glasses on a string round his neck. He was standing in front of his younger son, Charlie, who sat on the edge of an armchair in the sitting room. The room had a violently patterned carpet and was very tidy.

"Tell them," Mr Atkins repeated.

Charlie said nothing, just looked at the floor.

"*Charles...*" his father started again.

"Dad, leave him," Ryan Atkins said. "He *can't* tell them."

Sam looked towards Ryan. Up till now the older boy hadn't said anything and Sam hadn't made reference to their meeting last night, though he was sure Ryan had recognised him.

"Of course he can tell them," Mr Atkins said. "If he knows who it was he can tell them."

"Yeah, and then what?" Ryan said, making it clear his father didn't get it. "Nothing's gonna happen, except next time they'll be looking for Charlie when there isn't a copper around. Then he'll get worse than a couple of bruises."

"Bruises? Can't you *see* his mouth?"

"I'm all right," Charlie said then. "I just– I just want to forget it. I don't know who he was."

Oz Sitwell shifted beside Sam.

"I'm afraid there's not a lot more we can do then," he said. "I'll make sure it's logged on our system though."

"What good will that do?" Mr Atkins said, unimpressed. "You know, this used to be a decent place to live when we first came here. Now there's gangs and drugs and vandalism, and that attack or whatever it was last night. And the police don't do anything to stop it."

"We do take every incident seriously," Oz said.

"Doesn't look like it to me," Mr Atkins said flatly.

As Mr Atkins closed the front door behind them, Oz took a moment to look both ways along the walkway. He checked the time, then made a note in his pocketbook.

"Is that it then?" Sam said.

"Probably." Oz put the pocketbook away. "Would you recognise him – the youth?"

"Yeah, definitely."

"Okay, well if you spot him again, sing out, okay?"

"But if Charlie won't make a statement..."

"I know, but if you see him there's no reason we shouldn't

make *his* life a bit more unpleasant, is there? Totally unconnected, of course."

Sam frowned. "How?"

"Oh, you'd be amazed," Oz said, then he tapped his clipboard. "Come on, we've still got the ground floor to do."

16.

BOOTH RESIDENCE
ESCOTT ROAD
13:21 HRS

"Lauren, do you know anyone who would have a reason to hurt Ashleigh?"

On the sofa next to her mother, Lauren Booth shook her head, but Holly could see that she was too worried, too nervous, for it to be true.

DS Woods obviously thought so, too.

"But she *was* in an argument with someone yesterday afternoon, wasn't she?" he asked.

Lauren shook her head again, looked away. "I don't know."

"I think you do," Woods said. "We've got a witness who saw you and Ashleigh with a lad called Drew Alford after school. They said Drew was threatening Ashleigh. Is that true?"

"No. No. I don't know," Lauren said.

Her father – who seemed to resent the intrusion into his living room on a Saturday afternoon – shifted on his feet. He and DS Woods were both standing.

"Listen," Mr Booth said. "If she says she doesn't know... I mean, what's this about? I know you said you thought Ashleigh'd been mugged but—"

"It's about a suspected rape," Woods cut in flatly. "We believe Ashleigh may have been sexually assaulted."

"Rape?" Colin Booth said. He sounded genuinely shocked, but Holly was watching Lauren – and when her father repeated the word Lauren seemed to cringe.

"Lauren, what do you know about Drew Alford?" Holly said. "You need to tell us."

Lauren was still for a moment, then when she spoke her voice was hushed and scared. "He was mad with Ash. He was saying stuff– He said...he said if she was going round spreading stuff about him she'd be sorry."

"What sort of stuff?" Holly asked. "You mean stories, or gossip?"

"I don't know. I didn't know what he meant." Lauren looked up. "He was really angry. Not shouting but just – just really wound up, kind of jabbing his finger. Do you know what I mean?"

"You mean he was threatening towards Ashleigh?" Woods asked.

Lauren nodded.

"Did he threaten you as well?"

"No." Lauren shook her head. "He didn't even look at me. It was Ash he was looking at, all the time."

"Where was this?"

"On the estate. Me and Ash were coming back here and he just came out of nowhere. It was like he'd been waiting or something. He comes up and he asks Ash if it's true what he's heard, that she's been saying things about him, and Ash just says she doesn't know what he's heard so she doesn't know if it's true."

"How did he react to that?"

"He didn't like it. He said something about how she shouldn't try and be clever with him. And then Ash said why, was he afraid he couldn't keep up? – That was when he really started to get mad. He called her a snotty bitch. He said she knew what he meant and if she wasn't careful she'd find out he wasn't so stupid."

"What did Ashleigh say to that?"

"Nothing. I mean, she just sort of gave him a look, then said 'Come on' to me and we walked away."

Woods looked up from his notebook. "So was that the end of it?"

Lauren nodded.

"Why didn't you tell us this before?"

"I don't know."

"Was it because you're afraid of Drew Alford?"

Lauren didn't say anything.

"Lauren? Tell them," her father insisted.

But as soon as he'd said it Lauren rounded on him. "Why? What do you know? If you'd taken her home like I asked you, instead of going out... But you couldn't be bothered, could you? You didn't care. Just cos she lives on the estate, just cos you think she's common."

"I don't!" her father said. "I never said that."

"Yes you did. You've said it dozens of times. You're

always making comments about her. You probably think she deserved it!"

"Lauren, stop it!" her mother cut in. "I know you're upset but—"

"You don't know anything!" Lauren said, turning on her now. "You're just as bad as him. You're always on his side. Nobody listens! Nobody ever listens to what – to what *I* say."

She pushed her mother's restraining hand aside and forced herself off the sofa, running from the room with a door slam behind her.

Her parents looked at each other for a moment.

"I'm sorry," Mrs Booth said then, turning to Woods. "I don't know what's the matter with her."

"I'll get her back," Mr Booth said, determined. "I'm not having her behaving like that, doesn't matter what's caused it."

He started towards the door, but Woods cut him off. "That's all right," he said. "She's obviously upset so maybe we should leave it for now. I'd still like to get a formal statement if she's willing to make one, but it can wait till she feels up to it. Maybe you could give me a call?"

Holly left the sitting room first, hoping that she'd find Lauren just outside. She wasn't there, but as Holly made her way to the hall she saw the girl sitting on the stairs.

"You all right?" Holly asked.

Lauren nodded but it was a small thing.

"Is there anything else you can tell me about yesterday?"

This time Lauren shook her head. "No," she said dully.

For a second Holly debated, then she said: "When Ashleigh left here yesterday she didn't go straight home. Do you know anywhere she might have gone, anyone she might have met? A boyfriend maybe?"

"No," Lauren said again. "I told you, she isn't like that. I mean, she's not into boys yet – not serious; not more than fancying someone in a band or whatever, you know?"

"So there's no one at school?"

"No."

"And not Drew Alford?"

"No. I told you. She thinks he's a moron."

Behind her Holly heard DS Woods and Lauren's father leaving the sitting room. When Lauren registered it too, she stood up. "Will you find out who did it?"

"We'll try," Holly said, knowing it didn't sound as positive as she'd have liked.

Lauren seemed about to say something more, but as she saw DS Woods coming along the hall she abandoned it and turned quickly to go up the stairs.

"Lauren..." her father called after her, but Lauren took no notice and a moment later they heard her bedroom door close with a dull thud.

17.

INCIDENT ROOM
MORNINGSTAR RD STATION
14:02 HRS

The afternoon quiet of the Incident Room made the place seem larger than it had that morning, when the activity had been concentrated and driven. Instead of uniform and CID officers coming and going, it was just the four of them now and Holly knew she was to blame for keeping the others away from whatever it was they'd rather have been doing on a Saturday afternoon.

Danny Simmons was already in the Incident Room when Holly and DS Woods entered. Then, about ten minutes later, DI Jackie Connors had arrived. She was about thirty-five, dressed down but still smart in a silk blouse and knee-length wool skirt. She noticed Holly as soon as she entered, but chose not to make any comment. Instead she had a short conversation with Ray Woods at the far end of the room, before returning to the whiteboards and examining the photograph of Drew Alford, which was now at the centre of the case details.

"Go on then," she said to Woods. "How's he fit?"

She moved to lean against a desk as Woods picked up a marker pen and drew on the board.

"Tamsin Powell – known as Taz – says she saw Drew Alford

threatening Ashleigh and Lauren Booth at about 16:00 hours yesterday on the Cadogan Estate. According to Tamsin, Alford might have thought that Ashleigh had been 'disrespecting' him."

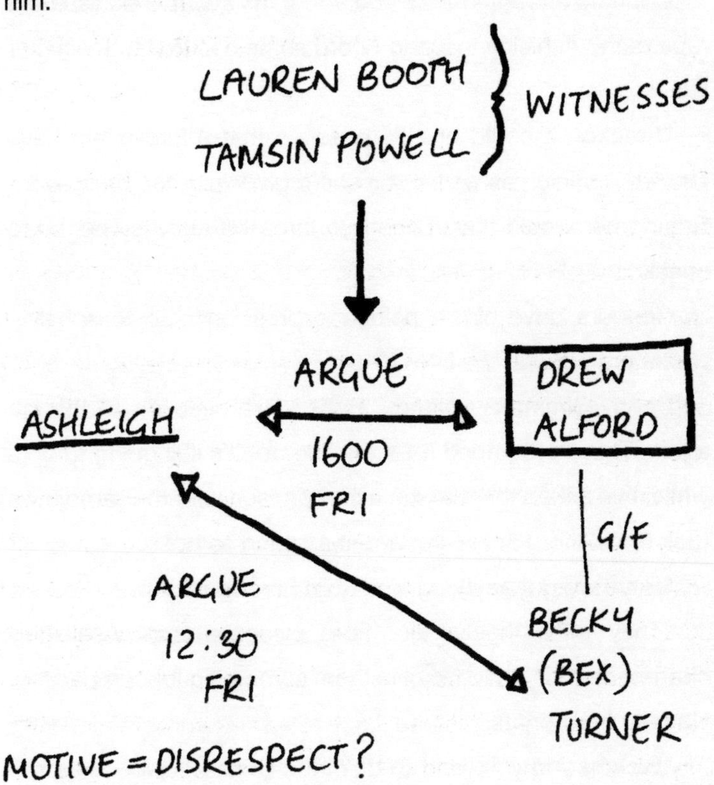

"Can we confirm that?" DI Connors asked. "If we're going to prove motive..."

Woods nodded. "Lauren Booth confirmed that Alford was angry because of things Ashleigh was supposed to have said about him. From the sound of it, Ashleigh might have made things worse when Alford confronted her. It sounds as if she gave him some lip and in return he called her a 'snotty bitch', amongst other things."

Connors assessed that. "So you think it was a punishment rape then? Ashleigh insulted Alford so he decided to teach her a lesson."

"I reckon it could be. It's possible that Alford might have fancied Ashleigh as well, but if she'd given him the brush off... Raping her would have been two birds with one stone, so to speak."

Connors gave him a pained expression. "So to speak – where are we with the DNA?"

Danny Simmons shifted. "Boss? I've been on to the lab again. They've bumped it up the line but it's still going to be a while. I've asked them to run a comparison with the sample we took from Alford at his first arrest as soon as poss."

"Have we got anything else from Forensics?"

"They think they've got fibre evidence from Ashleigh's clothes, but we'd have to give them something for comparison. Nothing from prints."

"So what do you want to do?" the DI asked Woods as she looked at the board. Holly didn't think she seemed particularly convinced by any of it.

"Like I said," Woods told her, "I think we've got enough to give Alford a tug on suspicion of Ashleigh's rape."

"You know a decent brief's going to say we can't even be sure there *was* a rape – not without an allegation – I'm assuming

Ashleigh hasn't come round and you've just forgotten to tell me."

"No. There's no change."

"So we *could* just wait for the DNA."

"We could," Woods said. "But then that could take us into tomorrow and it gives Alford more time to concoct an alibi, maybe get rid of any clothing he was wearing."

"If it *was* him."

Connors considered for a moment longer, then she said: "Okay, see if he's at home. If he is, try and get him to come in voluntarily. If not..."

"Right," Woods said.

Connors nodded, then straightened up from the desk she'd been leaning on and looked at her watch. "I need to get to Tesco before they run out of everything decent."

"Spaghetti bolognese or risotto?"

"Risotto." She gave him a frown. "How did you know?"

"Cos it's always one or the other."

"No it's not."

Woods gave her a look.

"Well excuse *me* for not being Delia Smith," Connors said, heavy on the sarcasm. "Let me know when you've talked to Alford, okay?"

"It won't interrupt the risotto?"

Connors gave him a narrow-eyed look, then turned and moved towards the door. Instead of heading out though, she stopped in front of Holly.

"TPO Blades, right?" she said. The easy banter she'd shared with Woods was gone and instead the DI seemed steely and stiffly formal.

"Yes, ma'am," Holly said and stood straight.

"Looks like you've buggered up everyone's Saturday."

"Yes, ma'am," Holly repeated, not sure what else to say.

"Right." And with a nod she continued on, out of the room, trailing perfume in her wake.

There was a moment of silence and then DS Woods said: "Danny, you up for the tug? I'm going to check through the statements from the door-to-door to see if there's any mention of Alford. Holly, you too."

"Sarge?" Holly wasn't sure what she was being told to do.

"Go with Danny," Woods said. "It's your info so you can put in the legwork to check it out." And with a last glance at the boards he started away.

"Come on then," Danny Simmons said to Holly. "Let's see how hard it is to find Mr Alford."

And as he gestured her towards the door, Holly felt the weight of responsibility for all this settling on her shoulders.

18.

PENRICE HOUSE
CADOGAN ESTATE
14:31 HRS

They rode up in the lift accompanied by the stench of a dirty nappy, despite the fact that Danny Simmons had kicked the offending article out into the lobby before the doors closed.

On the fifth floor they made their way along the walkway, passing one or two people who didn't bother to conceal their interest in the two coppers. A couple of men in their twenties saw them coming and immediately left their position at the railing to dodge back inside a flat and close the door. As he passed the same door a moment later Danny Simmons gave it a kick and said loudly, "Not today, Ricky. You got lucky – for once."

There was no response from the flat.

A few metres further on the door of flat 516 was also closed, its paint shabby and in need of attention. Danny Simmons waited until Holly was behind him, then banged on the door with the side of his fist.

For a moment there was nothing, then an unintelligible voice was raised inside. Simmons thumped the door again. "Police! Open up please."

Finally, after a full thirty seconds, the door was opened by a woman in her thirties. She had a washed-out complexion and blonde hair whose roots were several weeks overdue for retouching. She wore jeans and a sweater and had a tea towel in her hand.

"Mrs Alford?" Danny Simmons asked.

"Yeah."

"I'm DC Simmons from Morningstar Road station, this is TPO Blades. We're looking for Drew. Is he in?"

"Why?" the woman said. She shifted her gaze to Holly, as if the only unusual thing about all this was her presence. Holly was glad she was back in full uniform again.

"I'd like to ask him a couple of questions," Simmons said. "If he's here."

"Only two of you? Last time it was half a dozen."

"We were hoping he might be a bit more cooperative this time," Simmons said without missing a beat. "Can we come in?"

The woman gave him a look, then said, "He's in his room."

She led them into the flat and Holly closed the door behind them. At the hallway leading to the bedrooms Mrs Alford stood aside and gestured. "Second on the left," she said. "And if you're gonna arrest him again don't ask me to come with him. I had enough of that last time."

"Is his dad here?" Simmons asked.

Mrs Alford shook her head. "Football, pub, more pub, chippy, home. He'll probably talk to you lunchtime tomorrow."

"Right."

Mrs Alford didn't bother to reply but went back to the kitchen, as if she wanted nothing to do with the consequences of disturbing her son.

When she'd gone Danny Simmons moved along the hall to Drew Alford's room. He knocked on the door, then tried the handle. It was locked.

"Drew? I'm DC Simmons from Morningstar Road station. I need to talk to you."

There was a moment of silence and then the sound of movement and urgent, hissed voices. Simmons knocked again, harder. "Now please."

"All right, all right, keep your hair on," Drew Alford's irritated voice called from inside the room. There was another muffled exchange inside the room and Holly thought the second voice sounded female. Then the door was unlocked and Drew Alford opened it.

He was tall, well muscled, with an unruly thatch of brown hair and an angular face beneath it. He was fastening a pair of jeans over boxer shorts and had a shirt in his hand. In the bed behind him a girl with dark hair and a heart-shaped face was rapidly pulling a black T-shirt down over her pink bra.

"Your mum didn't say you'd got company," Simmons said, looking from Alford to the girl. "Hope we're not interrupting."

"Not now, you're not," Alford said.

"Like to introduce us?"

Alford shrugged and looked over his shoulder to the girl. "What's your name again?"

The girl, already uncomfortable at the intrusion, made a face. "Fuck off, Drew," she said.

"I thought I already did," Alford said with a grin.

"What's your name, love?" Simmons said, cutting through the banter.

"Bex."

"Bex? Okay, you don't need to come. This is TPO Blades. She'll stay with you, okay? – Come on, Drew, do yourself up through there."

With a sour look, Drew Alford zipped up his jeans and went along the hall towards the sitting room. As he did so Simmons leaned in towards Holly, dropping his voice.

"Bex?" he said significantly. "Have a chat, yeah?"

Holly knew what he meant and as Simmons moved off along the hall Holly went into the bedroom. Bex was pushing her hair back from her face.

"Can you shut the door?" she asked.

Holly did that and then Bex swung her legs out of bed and started hunting on the floor for the rest of her clothes. She was only dressed from the waist up.

Holly looked round the room to give the girl some privacy and also to give herself some time to think about what to say next. The room smelled of stale cigarette smoke and there was an ashtray on the floor with what might have been the remains of two or three spliffs in amongst the other dog-ends. On the walls there were several posters of topless models and some football stuff but nothing to indicate that

Drew Alford knew the meaning of tidy.

By now Bex had found her knickers and a pair of jeans. As she pulled the jeans on she glanced at Holly and said, "Is he in trouble again – Drew?"

"I don't know," Holly said, adopting a slightly fed-up air. "They never tell me anything. I mean, they tell me what to do, but not why."

This didn't seem to surprise or interest Bex.

"Is his mum out there?" she said, with a nod at the door.

"Yeah. She let us in."

"Shit."

"What's up? Don't you like her?"

"She don't like me," Bex said, looking for a sock to match the one in her hand. "Drew said she wouldn't be back till later or I wouldn't've come. She's a real cow – you seen a sock like this?"

Holly moved round the bed to look. "Have you been going out with him long?" she asked casually.

"Three months nearly."

"Long time," Holly said. "Do you live near here?"

"Yeah, Cranham House. It's a dump."

"I don't suppose you saw anything around the flats last night did you, about half past six? We're supposed to ask anyone we meet today if they were in the area."

"Nah, I was down the High Street till eight," Bex said, a note of resentment coming into her voice. She gestured towards the sitting room. "*He* was supposed to meet me at seven but he wouldn't answer his phone, just leaves me standing out in the cold like a numpty. Dickhead."

"Right," Holly said, keeping her tone light. "So he stood you up?"

Bex nodded. "He can be a real tosser sometimes."

"They all can," Holly said. "Oh, here you go."

She picked up the missing sock and held it out to the other girl.

"Ta."

Bex sat on the bed to pull on the sock and looked at Holly. "So how long's he gonna be? I'm not sitting round waiting if it's gonna be ages."

"Hold on," Holly said. "I'll see if I can find out."

"See if his mum's there an' all, yeah?"

"Okay, stay here," Holly said and moved to the door.

In the corridor there was no sign of Mrs Alford, but as Holly went along to the sitting room she could hear the conversation between Drew Alford and Danny Simmons. She stopped in the doorway, not wanting to interrupt. Alford had his back to her, perched on an armchair, and although she knew Danny Simmons could see her, he didn't look her way.

"Listen, I don't even know what's supposed to have happened, right?" Alford was saying. "So how can I have had something to do with it?"

"I didn't say you did," Simmons said. "But someone gave us your name and said they'd seen you on the estate at the right time."

Holly knew this wasn't entirely accurate, but even she couldn't tell that Danny Simmons was stretching the truth.

"Yeah, well, I live here don't I?" Drew Alford said. "I'm always around."

"That must be why we get so many complaints," Simmons said, and without waiting for a response he glanced towards Holly.

Drew Alford twisted his neck to look, then made to stand up.

"Stay put," Simmons told him.

He crossed to Holly and they retreated to the hall.

"Bex says she was supposed to be meeting him last night at about seven," she told Simmons in a low voice. "He didn't show up though, and he wasn't answering his phone."

"That's useful. Okay, let's see if he'll come nicely."

Holly followed Danny back to the sitting room and when Alford saw her again he made no attempt to disguise the fact that he was looking her over. It felt like he was appraising her – as if he had every right to look at her that way if he pleased.

He's always saying stuff like "She's a three, she's an eight". That was what Taz had said, and now Holly knew it must be true. She had to make a determined effort not to react.

"Okay, Drew," Danny Simmons said. "I'd like you to come to the station so we can talk about this on the record."

"What if I don't want to?" Alford said, finally looking away from Holly. "I told you, I ain't done nothing."

"So you shouldn't object to helping us eliminate you from

the investigation. But if you do…" He let the alternative hang in the air, unspoken but clear.

Alford took a second or two, then gave an exaggerated sigh. "All right," he said. "If you want to waste your time."

"Right, you'd better find some shoes and a coat then. I'll tell your mum what's happening."

"Don't bother," Alford said. "She couldn't care less."

19.

INTERVIEW ROOM 2
MORNINGSTAR RD STATION
15:18 HRS

In the Observation Room Danny Simmons was trying to find a working biro amongst the half-dozen scattered across the desk. He tried them on a pad, one by one, and when they failed to work he tossed them into the bin. After he'd done this six times Holly couldn't stand it any more and handed him one from her pocket.

"Here," she said, then added: "I've got a clean hankie too, if you need it."

"Thanks, Mum."

Holly chuckled. "I thought you'd be in there," she said then, gesturing to the interview room on the TV monitor.

"Ray Woods puts a bit more weight behind it," Simmons said. "A DS rather than DC. And it's easier to make notes where the suspect can't see you. That way they can't pick up on the things you're most interested in."

"Sneaky," Holly said.

"No point giving them any help."

He glanced at the monitor which now showed Drew Alford being ushered into the interview room next door and directed to a chair at the table. The main part of the screen was focused on Alford's seat, but in the upper right-hand corner there was a wider view, showing the entire interview room.

Holly watched Alford closely for a moment as he sat down at the table. She tried to match what she saw against what they thought he'd done. The trouble was, she knew her perception was coloured by everything else. Were his angular, unforgiving features and sullen expression really an indication of guilt, or would she have thought nothing of them if she'd caught sight of him on the bus or in the street? She couldn't tell.

"You know how this works?" Danny asked. "Have you done interview techniques?"

"Not really, just taking statements."

"It's not that different – well, actually, yeah, it is." He thought for a moment, then gestured at the monitor. "Basically Ray will get him to give an account of what he was doing yesterday. Doesn't matter if he says he was having tea with the Queen – once he's said it we've got it on record, so when we start to prove he was doing something else we've got the advantage. He has to explain why he lied."

"What if he just comes out and admits it straight away?"

"We get to knock off early and go to the pub. He won't though."

"How do you know?"

Danny gestured at the screen. "Look at his body language, the way he's sitting."

On the screen Holly saw that Alford had his arms folded and

was leaning back, as if to distance himself from the others in the room.

"They call that a closed posture," Danny said. "No way we're getting to the pub for a bit."

And as DS Woods took a seat in the interview room, Danny Simmons pressed a button on the monitor to bring up the sound.

"I'm Detective Sergeant Woods, attached to Morningstar Road station. The time is now 15:21 on Saturday February 5th and we are in Interview Room 2 at Morningstar Road station. I'm talking to – say your full name for the tape please, Drew."

"Drew Thomas Alford."

"Also present is—"

"Clare Hennessey, social worker acting as appropriate adult."

"Thank you. – Drew, you know that you're not under arrest and you're free to leave at any time, is that correct?"

"Yeah."

"Good. So you do not have to say anything, but it may harm your defence if you do not mention when questioned something which you later rely on in court. Anything you do say may be given in evidence. Do you understand?"

"Yeah, yeah," Alford said. "But this ain't going to court cos I didn't do nothing. Okay? So can we get on with it?"

With the formalities over, Ray Woods took a moment and leaned back in his chair. Finally he said: "Okay, I'm going to be straight with you. We're investigating a serious incident – an assault – that happened between six and seven o'clock last night near Drury House. The victim was a girl called Ashleigh Jarvis and we have witnesses who say that someone matching your description was in the area where we think the assault took place. Have you got anything to say to that?"

For a moment Alford looked at the table in front of him, then he shook his head. "No," he said flatly. "They're wrong."

"Okay," Woods said. "We also have witnesses who say you had an argument with Ashleigh yesterday afternoon. Is that true?"

"No."

"Okay. So can you tell me where you were between six and seven o'clock last night?"

Alford seemed to consider it, then he said: "At the offie."

"An off-licence?"

"Yeah."

"Which one?"

"On Reynolds Road."

"Was anyone with you?"

"Yeah. Tyler and Skank, some others. Ask them if you want, they'll tell you."

"How long were you there?"

Alford shrugged. "Dunno. An hour, maybe a bit more."

"Doing what? That seems like a long time to be in a shop."

"We weren't in it, were we? Round the side. It's where we go. Hang out."

"Right, I see," Woods said, as if it was all becoming clear.

"So you were at the off-licence and then what? Where did you go after that?"

"Home."

"What time was that, when you got home?"

Another shrug. "About seven. I don't know. I didn't look."

"How long would it take to get to your flat from the off-licence on Reynolds Road do you think? Ten minutes?"

"I suppose."

"Okay," Woods said with a nod. "So let's assume you got home at seven and it took you ten minutes. That would mean you left the off-licence at ten to seven, and if you were there for about an hour you must have arrived at about ten to six. Would you say that was true?"

"Probably." Alford shifted. "Listen, that proves I didn't have nothing to do with it, right? With what happened to her."

"It might," Woods said. "We'll have to ask the others if they can back it up though."

"Ask them then, they'll tell you."

"There you go," Danny Simmons said, glancing up from his notes to see if Holly had followed what was said. "That's his account: 'I was at the offie with Tyler and Skank from six till seven.' He's locked in."

"You mean if he admits to anything different it proves he was lying?" Holly asked.

"Yep. And the more different versions he gives the worse it looks if it goes to court."

"I get it," Holly said. "*If you didn't tell the truth about that, how do we know you're telling the truth about this?*"

Simmons nodded. "It's all about how it looks to a jury."

Then his phone chirped and he picked it up to look at the text.

"DNA results are in," he said, standing up. "Think you can keep notes while I go and pick up the email?"

"Er, yeah, sure," Holly said. "Just the main points, right?"

"Yeah. I'll be back in five."

As he opened the door Holly looked at the monitor, then wheeled her chair around in front of it.

As if thinking it all through DS Woods made a note on his pad. Without looking up he said casually: "So tell me how you know Ashleigh Jarvis."

"I don't. I've seen her in school, that's all."

"But you know who she is?"

"Yeah. I just said. She's at school."

"Did you see her or talk to her on Friday?"

"No."

"Not at all?"

"No."

"What about Lauren Booth? Do you know her?"

"Yeah."

"Did you see her on Friday?"

"No."

"Are you sure?"

"I just said, didn't I?"

"What about on the estate, around four o'clock?"

"What about it?"

"Well, when we talked to Lauren she said you approached her and Ashleigh as they were walking home."

Alford didn't speak immediately. He kept his arms folded and his gaze on the table in front of him. Finally he said: "Okay, so I saw them."

"You talked to them?"

"So?"

"What about?"

Alford shrugged. "Can't remember."

Woods shifted slightly. "Lauren told us there was an argument, between you and Ashleigh. Is that true?"

"No."

Woods looked at his notes. "You didn't say that Ashleigh was a 'snotty bitch'?"

"No."

"Are you sure? Why would Lauren say that if it wasn't true?"

"She don't like me."

"Oh? Why not?"

"Don't know, do I?"

"What about Ashleigh? Does she like you?"

"Dunno."

"Do you like her?"

Alford shrugged.

"Do you fancy her?"

"No." He said it as if the idea was an insult.

"So why did you talk to them? I mean, if you think Lauren doesn't like you and you don't fancy Ashleigh..."

"I just saw them, that's all."

"Was it because you thought Ashleigh had been disrespecting you and you wanted to have it out with her?"

"Who says that?" Alford said resentfully.

"Several people we've talked to. They all seem to think you were annoyed because Ashleigh had said something disrespectful about you."

"I don't know." Alford folded his arms tighter across his chest.

"You don't know what she said?" Woods asked. "I thought it was pretty common knowledge. Didn't she say she wouldn't want to have sex with you because she thought you'd got herpes or Aids? Didn't she say she thought you were a tosser?"

The DS leafed back through his notes as if he might have got it wrong and needed to be sure. "Wasn't that what she said – 'a tosser'? – Yeah, it's here. She said you were a tosser."

Woods looked back to Alford. "So if she's calling you names and saying you've got herpes or Aids..."

"Listen!" Alford snapped angrily. "I told her to keep her mouth shut, all right? That was all." He leaned forward and jabbed a finger at Woods for emphasis. "I told her and then I walked off. I didn't have nothing to do with anything else and you can fuck off if you think I did."

"Okay, Drew, calm down," Woods said, unmoved by the

outburst. "She insulted you and you didn't like it. That's fair enough."

"Yeah? Well, she shouldn't have said it, that's all. But that don't mean I did anything else. I told you where I was. I wasn't nowhere near her." He gave it a moment to emphasise the point, then sat back and folded his arms again as if that was his last word on the subject.

Then, from the speakers, Holly heard a knock on the interview room door and on the monitor she saw it open a short way. She couldn't see or hear what was said, but after a moment Woods turned back to face Alford.

"We need to take a break," he said. "Shouldn't be more than five minutes. Is that okay?"

Alford shrugged.

"Okay. Interview suspended at 15:33. Ms Hennessey will stay with you. Would you like a drink?"

The observation room door opened behind Holly and Danny Simmons came in.

"What's going on?" she asked.

"DNA," he said, moving to stop the recording equipment.

"Is it his?"

"Yes and no."

20.

INCIDENT ROOM
MORNINGSTAR RD STATION
15:44 HRS

"They ran profiles on three samples," Danny Simmons said. He was writing on the whiteboard at the same time. "There's the semen found internally by the rape exam, a pubic hair also from the rape kit, and a head hair from Ashleigh's coat. The head hair doesn't match anyone – not Ashleigh, not Alford. The pubic hair does though. It's Alford's. It matches on sixteen alleles, so it's definite."

"And the semen?"

"No match."

"Bollocks," Ray Woods said.

"Yeah, well it came from someone's, just not Alford's."

Woods let out a heavy, frustrated sigh. "So where's that leave us? What's going on?"

He looked at the board.

Head hair = Unknown
Pubic hair = Alford
Semen = Unknown

"Alford must have had sexual contact with Ashleigh for his

pube to be there, so how come it's not his semen? – Could there have been two of them? Alford and someone else?"

Holly had a thought. "What if Alford used a condom and the other one didn't? Or maybe Alford didn't – er…" She stumbled and felt herself flush when she realised what she'd been about to say. "Didn't *finish*."

She felt the heat in her face intensify as the two men looked at her.

Woods shifted. "Maybe you could find us a coffee while we talk about this?" he suggested.

"Sarge, I *do* know the facts of life," Holly said, determined not to be beaten by her discomfort, or to be sidelined because of it.

Woods took a moment, then glanced at Danny Simmons who just shrugged. It seemed to be enough.

"Okay," Woods said. "I'm just going to pretend you're twenty-six, okay? So don't expect any soft soap."

"I think I can cope," Holly said.

"I think she can, too," Danny Simmons added matter-of-factly.

"Right, so – this." Woods tapped the board to bring them back to the subject. "We think there could have been two of them. Alford uses a condom, the other one doesn't."

"Actually, I think we're wrong about two suspects," Danny said, scanning the report. "There's no trace of spermicide from a condom according to the lab, and the breakdown in the semen sample indicates that it was at least six hours old at the time of the rape exam and could have been present for up to twenty-four hours."

"Have they left any other little surprises in there for us?" Woods asked tartly, with a nod at the paper.

"No, that's it."

"Huh," Woods said, and then wrote *6-24 hours old* next to *Semen Unknown*.

"So Ashleigh had had sex with an unknown male at some point in the previous twenty-four hours. That *could* be our rape or it could have been consensual, but it wasn't Alford."

"That still doesn't let him off the hook though, does it?" Holly said. "He must've done something to Ashleigh last night, otherwise how do we explain his pubic hair?"

"How does *he* explain it?" Woods said. "That's more to the point."

21.

INTERVIEW ROOM 2
MORNINGSTAR RD STATION
16:13 HRS

"No. Look, what's this got to do with anything? I've told you where I was. I want to pack this in now. I've had enough."

Alford pushed his chair back and stood up. Ray Woods didn't react. Instead he peeled back the wrapper from a tube of throat soothers and as he did so he said: "You've missed something out though, haven't you, Drew?"

"No."

Woods put a sweet in his mouth, sucked for a moment, then lodged it in his cheek. "Yes you have. You haven't told us about meeting Ashleigh."

"Yeah I did."

Woods shook his head. "I don't mean when she was with Lauren. I mean later, when she was alone – when she was walking home across the estate from Lauren's house." He looked up at Alford. "Want to sit down and tell me about that before you go?"

Alford took a moment, then reluctantly sat back down on the chair.

"I never saw her. I told you, I was at the offie."

"I know that's what you said, but it doesn't explain why our forensic scientists found your DNA on Ashleigh."

"They can't have. It's not mine."

"Oh, it is. It's a definite match."

Alford shrugged. "So maybe it was from when I talked to her earlier."

"Must've been a strange conversation – for one of your pubic hairs to get itself into Ashleigh's knickers." He looked flatly at Alford.

Drew Alford scowled but said nothing.

Woods waited several seconds, then he said: "You're king of the hill, aren't you, Drew? On the estate. So when Ashleigh said something that disrespected you, you were angry. You had to do something about it. You had to put her in her place."

"No comment."

"So when you saw her on her way home you attacked her. You took her into the bin shelter and you sexually assaulted her."

"No comment."

"So explain it for me," Woods said, unruffled. "Explain to me how one of your pubic hairs came to be on Ashleigh Jarvis if you *didn't* sexually assault her."

Drew Alford took a moment, then sniffed. "Cos she wanted it, that's how."

In the observation room Holly tensed, then leaned in to see the monitor better.

"Okay..." Woods said, his voice flat and even. "So tell me what happened."

Alford said nothing for a moment and Holly could tell he was rehearsing his story in his head, getting it straight. Finally he unfolded his arms and sat forward.

"I saw her," he said. "I'm going home and I see her. Then she sees me and she comes over."

"Ashleigh came to you?"

"Yeah."

"What time was that?" Wood said.

"I dunno. 'Bout quarter to seven. I didn't look."

"Okay, go on."

"So she says she's sorry about what she said before. She says she just said it cos Bex was having a go at her about something. Then she asks if I'm serious about her."

"Serious about who – Bex?"

"Yeah."

"So what did you say?"

"I said no. I said it was just a thing, right? Bex isn't nothing special. So then Ash asks me if I think *she's* special. She says, 'You think I'm a ten?' And I say I reckon she's a nine."

In the observation room Danny Simmons snorted. "Great chat-up line."

Holly took no notice. She was watching the monitor closely as Drew Alford leaned forward a little more.

"So she says, 'I'm a ten. You want me to show you?' And I said sure. So she says, 'Let's go over there, where it's private,' and we go over to the bin shelter. That's where she starts snogging me, right? I'm telling you, she's the one doing it all –

snogging me, rubbing up, right? You know what I mean. She says she's fancied me for ages but didn't want no one to know." He looked directly at Woods. "Listen, I'm telling you straight, right? It was all her idea, not mine. But I wasn't gonna say no, was I?"

"Because you fancied her?"

"Yeah, sure, I suppose."

Woods nodded. "So then what happened?

"She's letting me, you know, touch her up, right? And she's touching me too, right? But then all of a sudden she goes all weird. She starts crying and shit, saying how she's changed her mind, it was a mistake. She doesn't want to do it."

"So what did you do?"

"Nothing." He saw Woods's dubious expression. "Listen, I'm telling you, it's true. I'm pissed off, aren't I? I know what she's doing – she's just prick-teasing. So I tell her she's a bitch or something, I can't remember, and then I tell her she's gonna get a rep: she wants to watch out."

"You didn't try to make her go through with what she'd started?"

"No, man. I ain't no— I don't need to force her, right? Why would I?"

"Because you were aroused?"

"No! Listen, I want a shag I just call Bex, right? I don't need that stuck-up bitch, Ashleigh. Why would I?"

Woods took a moment, then said: "So who left the bin shelter first, you or Ashleigh?"

"Her. She pushes past me and goes."

"How long after she'd gone did you leave?"

"I dunno, a minute or two."

"And when all this happened there was only you and Ashleigh there, is that right?"

"Yeah, I told you."

"When you left did you see anyone else?"

Alford hesitated, but only for a fraction of a second. "No."

"And where did you go?"

"Home."

"So when we ask Ashleigh about this, she's going to confirm what you've said? She's going to tell us that you didn't try to force her to have sex with you?"

"She'd better, cos if she doesn't she's lying. No way I did that. No way."

Woods seemed to consider that for a second or two, then without any trace of emotion he said, "Okay, Drew, you've been very helpful. I'm going to terminate this interview now and have a chat with my colleagues, okay?"

"So I can go, right?" Alford said.

"No, I'll need you to wait. Interview terminated at 16:21."

22.

MORNINGSTAR RD STATION
INCIDENT ROOM
16:43 HRS

"He's charm on a stick, isn't he?"

DI Connors pressed a button on the remote and stopped the playback of Alford's interview.

"Can't nick him for that though." She gestured at the whiteboards. "Can't nick him for this, either."

"Sure?" Woods asked.

"Has Ashleigh come round?"

"No."

"So there's no complainant and there's no firm evidence of rape or even attempted rape. Assault… Maybe. Just. – No, not even that."

"Okay," Woods said, accepting it. "Just wanted to be sure."

Holly took a half-step forward.

"Ma'am – she did have scratches on her thighs. And if she hadn't been scared of Alford, trying to get away from him, I don't think she'd have left her coat, shoes and bag in the bin shelter."

She looked to Woods for confirmation, but when she saw his expression she knew she'd made a mistake.

"*If* Alford made the scratches," Connors said. "*If* he did so intending harm rather than in the heat of passion when he tried to feel her up. *If* she left the shelter in fear rather than in a hurry to catch the Number 10 bus. *If*—"

But clearly she'd got tired of the *if*s and waved it all away before turning back to DS Woods.

"Send him home. We've got his statement. If things change we can go back to it, but we're not going to get anything else until or unless Ashleigh tells us what was going on. Pack this up till Monday. We'll need to see what it's done to the budget, too. Now, I'm going home to cook. And it's *not* risotto: it's poached salmon, new potatoes, mixed salad and dressing. Eight thirty. Don't be late."

"Not with that menu," Woods said.

Connors nodded, then turned to leave. As she did so she gestured Holly to go with her. They went as far as the corridor before Connors stopped again and turned to her.

"Just so you know: initiative's one thing; trying to run before you can walk is another. Right?"

The flat put-down was even harder than Holly had expected.

"Yes, ma'am. I didn't mean to—"

"There aren't any short cuts, okay?" the DI said, cutting her off. "I don't like the TPO scheme. I think you're all too young for the job, even if you are supposed to be potential high-fliers. There's a time and a place for training and in my opinion CID isn't it – and we don't need a mascot. You understand what I'm saying?"

"I—" Holly started to say, then bit her tongue. "Yes, ma'am," she said.

Connors nodded. "Right, as long as we're clear," and she headed away.

23

Through the thin bedroom wall Ryan heard the bathroom door close and lock. By the time he'd finished texting Dav the shower had started to run. It was the regular Saturday evening ritual: his father got ready to go to the club for a few hours – the only night of the week he ever did go out.

Now he was sure that his father was occupied, Ryan swung his legs off the bed and pocketed his phone. He made his way down the hall to the sitting room and found Charlie scrolling through a game menu on the Xbox. He looked up when Ryan entered.

"Want to race?" he asked, holding out the second controller.

Ryan shook his head.

"You going out?"

"Maybe. In a bit," Ryan said. "So who was it? And don't say you don't know, cos I know you do."

Charlie knew what he was talking about and couldn't help running his tongue over the cut on his lip. "I don't," he said, shaking his head.

"Listen," Ryan said. "I can't do anything if you don't tell me."

"You don't need to do anything," Charlie said. "It was just…"

"Was it the Kaddys? Cos if it was—"

"No," Charlie said, then realised he'd said it too quickly. "I told you, I never saw him before. And anyway, you don't need to do anything. I can look after myself. I'm not a kid."

"Yes you are," Ryan said flatly.

The bluntness of the statement stung Charlie, made worse because Ryan had always been able to look after himself. His lack of fear and his certainty that he could handle whatever came along just seemed to be instinctive. It was something that Charlie knew would never come naturally to him, no matter how much he wished for it.

"It doesn't matter," Charlie said. "It's only a cut. It's nothing."

Ryan held his eye for a second longer, then shrugged dismissively. "Okay," he said. "Please yourself. I was only trying to help."

"I know," Charlie said, because he knew it was true – and because he didn't want Ryan to think he didn't care. He held out the second game controller again. "Have one race, okay? Till Dad goes out."

Ryan hesitated for a moment. Then he shifted and took the handset because he could see that Charlie wanted them to be mates again. "I choose the circuit then," he said, taking a seat.

24.

MORNINGSTAR RD STATION

17:21 HRS

Sam and Oz were waiting when Holly escorted Drew Alford out of the custody cage into the yard and right away Sam could tell she wasn't happy. She was straight-faced and walked stiffly as she accompanied Alford the short distance to the patrol car.

Oz Sitwell had clearly picked up on Holly's demeanour too. "Doesn't look like our Hol's having much fun playing for the other side," he said.

"No," Sam agreed, and a small bit of him wasn't unhappy about that. He knew it was mean-spirited, but he couldn't help feeling jealous that Holly had managed to get herself on the inside of the investigation while he had been stuck on the boring and unproductive door-to-door enquiries.

"All right, Drew?" Oz said, shifting. "Going home without charges? Must be your lucky day."

"Yeah, well that's cos I didn't do anything," Alford said.

"Listen—" Holly said sharply. Then she stopped herself, but not before Sam saw something in her expression that he hadn't seen before. It was a flash of genuine anger that made her look surprisingly dangerous – not at all what he was used to, but not unattractive.

"We'll talk to you again when Ashleigh comes round," Holly told Alford, her voice more measured.

"Please yourself," Alford said, then turned to Oz. "So are we going or what?"

"Back seat," Oz said, and he stepped forward to open the car door.

Holly didn't move as Alford got in, and it was only when Oz swung the door closed with a thud that she turned on her heel and headed back into the nick.

From the observer's seat Sam kept an eye on Alford in the rear-view mirror while Oz pulled out of the yard and drove them towards the Cadogan Estate. As soon as they moved off Alford started texting on his phone. When he finished he sat and looked out of the window, like he was in the back of a taxi. If he was disturbed by his experience in the station Sam could see no sign of it.

Once they reached the Cadogan Estate Oz pulled in to the kerb outside Penrice House, then turned in his seat to speak to Alford.

"You want us to come up to the flat with you?" he said, but with no apparent intention of doing so.

"No."

"Okay. On your way then. And don't forget you'll have a court date coming up on that robbery charge."

"I didn't do that neither," Alford said.

"Course not," Oz said.

The rear door was security locked and couldn't be opened from inside, so Sam got out and pulled the handle. When Alford climbed out he headed straight across the road towards the flats without a word.

"So what do you reckon?" Sam asked, getting back into the car.

Oz considered for a moment. "If he didn't do it this time we'll get him for something else in the end," he said. "Sometimes you've got to play the long game. Although if he was smart he'd know that's how he could get away with it."

"How do you mean?" Sam asked, puzzled.

"Cos if he was smart he'd think, *They're going to be waiting for me next time, so I'll be clever – I won't give them a next time.* – But he'd have to be smart and he's not: see? Straight back in."

Oz gestured and, in the light of a street lamp on the far side of the road, Sam saw three teenage lads appear from beneath a concrete walkway and head towards Alford. One was distinctly bigger than the others, with blond hair. Sam squinted.

"I think that's the one who attacked Charlie Atkins," he said. "The one on the right – blond."

Oz looked, then pulled the car round a little way, flicking the headlights on to full beam so they illuminated the three youths.

"Yeah, that's definitely him," Sam said.

"Tyler Smith," Oz said. "Okay, that figures."

In the headlights Alford and the others shielded their eyes for a moment, then Alford gestured for them to move. Together they disappeared from sight amongst the shadows of the concrete columns.

"You don't want to pick him up?" Sam asked.

"No, we'll get back," Oz said, checking the wing mirror, then pulling out onto the road. "It'll be knock-off by the time we get there. Like I said: play the long game. Same as you and Bob Mulvey."

"What?"

Oz gave him a canny glance. "He was pretty pleased with himself last night, finding the scene of crime."

Instinctively Sam opened his mouth to speak, then closed it again.

"Right," Oz said shrewdly. "That's what I thought."

"Did Holly tell you?"

Oz shook his head. "I know Mulvey," he said, as if that explained everything.

25

"They talked to any of you?" Alford said, looking round the others suspiciously.

Standing in a half circle by the fence around the recreation area they all shook their heads: Tyler, Skank, Rizza.

"Yeah? Well someone's tried to drop me in it," Alford said, unconvinced.

"What did they want to know?" Skank asked.

"Where I was, what I was doing." Alford looked round the others again, gauging their reactions. "So you know what you say if they come back, right? All of us were down Jak's offie, like I told you last night."

More nods, but this time Alford caught a slight distraction from Tyler.

"What?" he said, zeroing in on the larger boy.

"What? Nothing," Tyler said, but there was an unmistakeable unease in the way he shifted from one foot to the other.

"You talked to them?" Alford said.

"Fuck off. No."

Alford eyed him suspiciously. He knew there was something Tyler was holding back, but before he could take it further Rizza cut in.

"So how come they reckon it's you – you know, raped whatshername – Ashleigh?"

Alford rounded on him swiftly. "They don't think it now cos it wasn't," he said sharply. "They know I never touched her. It was all bollocks and anyone says it was me again they're gonna get fucking done. Anyone. Right?"

Rizza nodded briskly to show he understood. No one was going to give Drew an excuse to kick off when he was in a mood like this – not even Tyler would risk that.

"Okay," Alford said, as if he was finally satisfied. "Anyway, she wouldn't know what to do with it if you put it in her hand. I wouldn't waste my time on it."

"I would," Skank said with a leer, and then he yelped as Alford's fist hit his ear.

"What the fuck! What you do that for?" His voice was a whine.

"Cos you're a fucking dickhead," Alford said. "You wanna get pulled in an' all cos someone says they heard you saying something like that? Have some fuckin' sense."

He pushed Skank in the chest and made him stagger backwards, then immediately turned and moved away from the fence.

"Where we going?" Rizza asked.

"Find Madder," Alford said. "I need a smoke."

26.

Danny Simmons drove in silence and made no attempt to get Holly to talk. She was glad about that because she wasn't sure what they'd talk about if it wasn't the case, and she didn't want to talk about that because – well – there was nothing to talk about now.

Outside the Section House Danny brought the car to a stop but left the engine running.

"There you go then," he said, giving the place the once-over through the window, then turning back to her.

"Thanks." Holly reached round and undid her seat belt.

"It goes that way sometimes," Danny said. "You think you've got it sorted and it all comes apart."

Holly knew he meant it as consolation so she nodded. "Thanks for letting me sit in," she said. "I learned a lot."

"Listen," Danny said, "it's Saturday night. You're off duty. Get a movie out, have a pizza, think about something else."

"What're you going to do?"

As soon as she said it Holly realised it had come out sounding halfway between an invitation and a request, which was not what she'd intended – even if it was how she felt.

"I mean, are you getting poached salmon with the DI as well?" she said, trying to cover.

"Me? Nah," Danny said, apparently oblivious. "Wouldn't

want to either. From what I hear, she's a crap cook. I mean, *really* crap. Ray has to go though – the DI's his sister-in-law."

"What? Really?"

"Yep."

"Harsh."

"Oh yeah," Danny said with a grin. "I'll see you later, okay?"

"Yeah," Holly said, returning the smile, then reaching for the door handle. "Thanks, Danny."

She stood on the pavement for a moment as his car pulled away, then saw Sam coming along the road towards the Section House. He was carrying his sports bag, his free hand shoved in his pocket.

"Who was that?" he said, gesturing after the car.

"Danny – DC Simmons."

"Oh. Right. You must be well in."

"It was just a lift," Holly said, suddenly irritated by the insinuation, and by the fact that he'd got it so wrong.

"Okay," Sam said with a shrug. "So what happened with Alford? Didn't he do it?"

"No. Yes. Sort of."

"What do you mean, 'sort of'?"

"Not now, eh?" Holly said. "I'm really tired."

"Okay, I was just asking." Sam swung his bag and moved towards the house.

Behind him Holly waited a moment, then pulled a breath before calling after him. "Sam, hold on – listen. You want to walk down the road for a pizza? I need to eat."

"Are you buying?"

"I bought yesterday and you still owe me."

"How much?"

"Two seventy."

"You sure?"

"Yes!"

The pizza place at the end of the road was brightly lit and more of a takeaway than a restaurant. There were three steel tables in the window where you could eat, though – if you didn't mind the draught from the coming and going of the delivery drivers.

Holly didn't. She just wanted to eat the pizza while it was hot, straight out of the box. But after only one mouthful she knew pizza wasn't really what she needed. She needed to say what was burning her up, even if Sam probably wasn't the ideal person to say it to.

"I just got a bollocking from the DI," she told him. "Connors."

"Why?" Sam looked surprised. "I thought—" he stopped himself.

"What?"

He shook his head. "Nothing – why?" he repeated.

"She reckoned I was trying to blag my way onto the enquiry – I mean into CID – because I didn't want to be on the cordon or something. She said I was trying to take a short cut, which I wasn't. Then she made a crack about them not needing a mascot."

She looked at him to see what his reaction was going to be, half prepared for some smart remark. Instead she became aware there was something different about the way he was looking at her.

"What?" she said.

"What?" Then he frowned. "But *you* got them the lead on Alford, right?"

"Yeah."

"So she should give you the credit."

"No chance with Connors," Holly said flatly. "She thinks TPOs are a waste of time."

"Sounds like she's related to Mulvey."

"Yeah, maybe. I don't really care about that, though. Well, I do but— It's just that they're all writing the case off: NFA. Nothing we can do, so drop it."

"But if the DNA proves Alford didn't rape Ashleigh—"

"He *tried* though. I'm sure of it. And that's why she ran under that truck. He's responsible for what happened to her but he's going to get away with it."

Sam nodded. It wasn't hard to see that Holly was genuinely frustrated by the injustice of it all, and he could understand that.

"Oz said something earlier, when we took Alford back to the estate," Sam told her. "He said he wasn't smart enough to keep out of trouble. He reckons we'll get him for something else – just a matter of time."

"Maybe," Holly said. Then she finally voiced what was really bugging her. "But even if you forget Alford it's still not sorted, is it? I mean, about what happened to Ashleigh."

"Why not?"

"Because everyone says she was quiet, didn't have many friends and wasn't into boys yet – she didn't even fancy anyone. But she'd had sex with *someone* before she was knocked down. So how's it fit? What *really* happened? Cos I don't think it's as simple as they're making out. I think there's something else going on."

"You could ask her when she comes round," Sam suggested. "That way you'd know."

Holly pursed her lips grimly. "You mean *if* she comes round," she said.

SUNDAY

1.

CUSTODY SUITE
MORNINGSTAR RD STATION
09:32 HRS

It wasn't true about there always being carrots in vomit. More often it was chunks of dodgy kebabs or yellow curry, especially on a Sunday morning after the Saturday night before. The drunks who'd been banged up the previous evening were given just long enough to sober up, then they were either charged or simply shown the door and left blinking in the cold morning light, trying to remember why drinking so much had seemed like fun.

As she mopped the floor of her third cell that morning Holly was glad of the smell of disinfectant, and that she had something to take her mind off what she was doing. The puzzle of what had really happened to Ashleigh Jarvis had been going round in her head when she'd woken up, and it was still there, still without an answer.

Once she'd finished cleaning up Holly put the mop and bucket back in the stores and went through into Custody where Sergeant Stafford was at the desk. He glanced up when she appeared, then gave her a knowing look. "Suppose you'll want refs now," he said, dryly. "Burger and chips, sausage and egg?"

"Think I might wait a bit if that's okay, Sarge," Holly said. "Is it all right if I go and wash my hands?"

"Yeah, we'll be quiet enough for a while now. When you've done that you can get some fresh air. Your pal Dr Scobie didn't give a statement about Ashleigh on Friday so you can go down to the Vic and get it now."

"Was that my fault?" Holly asked, hoping it wasn't.

"No, you're in the clear. It just got missed because he went off duty."

"Oh. Right. Good – I mean, I'm glad it wasn't me."

Stafford gave her a narrow-eyed look and Holly cursed herself for saying what she'd been thinking.

"I didn't get chance to ask you about working with CID yesterday," Stafford said. "How did that go?"

"It was fine, Sarge," Holly said. "Really interesting."

"*Just* interesting?"

"Yes, Sarge."

Stafford studied her for a moment longer, as if he knew exactly what she wasn't saying. Finally he just nodded.

"Okay, since you're going out there's a bag of Ashleigh Jarvis's personal effects to go back to her mother. You can collect it from Property then call to find out where Mrs Jarvis is – with any luck she'll be at the Vic too. Blag a lift with someone so it doesn't take all day."

"Yes, Sarge." She started to move off.

"Holly."

"Sarge?"

"A pearl of wisdom: decent coppers care about the victims; objective coppers catch villains. The best ones do both – get it?"

Holly thought about it, then nodded because she did. "So which are you, Sarge?"

"Me?" Stafford shook his head. "I'm an *old* copper. We're all bitter and twisted, so we don't count."

2

Ryan Atkins had his own routine for Sunday mornings, and part of it was staying out of the way until he heard the door close when Charlie and his dad left for church. By not showing his face he didn't give his father any opportunity to try and badger him into going with them. It was easier than having the same old confrontation all over again:

"Come to church."

"I don't *do* church."

"Why not? What's more important – lying in bed or showing your faith? If your mother was here..."

And so on and so on and so on...

What his father couldn't or wouldn't accept was that Ryan just didn't buy that stuff any more: *Jesus is love; turn the other cheek; the meek shall inherit the earth*. As far as Ryan could see, just living on the Cadogan Estate proved all that was bullshit, and if you thought it didn't you were just conning yourself.

So, even though he was awake, Ryan was still in bed when his phone rang. It was Dav.

"What's up?" Ryan said.

"You seen your car, man?"

"What car?"

"Your dad's. A blue one, right? Least it was."

"What the fuck you talking about?"

"You need to look, man," Dav said. "I'm down here now."

Ryan pulled on his jeans and a sweatshirt and pushed his bare feet into his trainers. Then he left his room and headed for the front door, passing his father in the kitchen, dressed in a suit and a tie.

"Ryan, where're you going?"

"I'll be back in a minute," Ryan said, opening the door. "I just need to see something."

Outside the wind was icy. He crossed the landing quickly to lean over the rail and look down. In the parking bay three floors below he saw exactly what Dav had been talking about. His father's dark blue Fiesta looked like something out of a comic book, with a large patch of white paint splashed over the roof and windscreen. Across the bonnet, where the white paint hadn't reached, a hasty, stick-like tag had been sprayed in yellow with no attempt at artistry: *KB*.

Dav was standing beside the car, looking up, and when he saw Ryan he made a pointless gesture towards it.

"Stay there, I'm coming down," Ryan called, and as he did so he sensed someone arrive next to him. When he turned he saw his father looking down at the same sight.

"Is that— That's *our* car!" Leyton Atkins said, with disbelief in his voice.

* * *

By the time Ryan had pulled on a pair of socks and a jacket and jogged down the stairs, Charlie and his father were already at the car. Dav had been joined by a tall, gangly boy called Tree and another called Simmo. All three were standing together, but not too close to the car, as if they wanted to make it clear they'd had nothing to do with the damage.

"Who'd do that?" Mr Atkins said as Ryan came to look more closely at the damage. "Why?"

Ryan said nothing. To him it wasn't a question that needed an answer.

Nearer the car, Charlie reached out and tested the white paint with his finger. The paint was still tacky but had obviously been there for some time. Charlie knew the answer to his father's question too, and it gave him an odd, hollow feeling in the pit of his stomach – part guilt and part anger.

"Don't get it on your suit," Mr Atkins told Charlie sharply. "Come away." He was taking his mobile from his pocket.

"Who're you calling?" Ryan asked.

"The police," Mr Atkins said. "Who else? I want to know who did this. I want them arrested."

Ryan knew from his father's tone that he was winding himself up to shout at someone. He glanced at the KB tag on the bonnet again, then back at his father. "The police won't know who did it."

"They can find out," Mr Atkins said with determination. "Decent people shouldn't have to put up with things like this. It's just mindless vandalism. I'm not going to let them get away with it."

"What about church?" Charlie said. "We'll be late if we don't go now and you can't drive the car like that."

His father paused, then looked at his watch.

"If you wait for the police it could be ages," Ryan said, pressing the point.

For a moment Leyton Atkins hesitated, then made up his mind.

"All right then, we'll walk," he said. "But as soon as service is over I'm calling the police. Whoever did this, they're not getting away with it, whoever they are." He looked at Ryan. "Are you staying here?"

Ryan nodded. "Yeah."

For a second it looked as if his father was going to argue about that too, but then he simply nodded and gestured to Charlie. "Come on, we'll need to get a move on."

As Charlie and his father strode off towards the road Ryan cast another look at the Kaddy Boys' tag on the car bonnet, then he moved to where Dav, Tree and Simmo were standing.

"You know who done that, don't you?" Tree said.

"No, who?" Ryan said sarcastically.

"They had to know it was yours," Dav said. "I mean, that's gotta be it – cos it's your dad's."

"Fucking Alford," Ryan said. "No way he's claiming this block. No fucking way. Cloudsley's ours."

"You reckon that's what he's trying to do?"

"Got to be, innit?" Simmo cut in. "What else?" He looked at Ryan to see if he'd agree.

Ryan thought about it for a moment, then he said: "Anyone seen them today – Alford's lot? Any of them?"

The others shook their heads.

"Okay, so we'll find them. I'm gonna sort this. I want to known what the fuck he thinks he's doing, then we decide how we handle it, okay?"

The others nodded.

"Okay then," Ryan said, determination hard in his voice, and he started away towards the centre of the estate.

3.

EMERGENCY DEPT
QUEEN VICTORIA HOSPITAL
09:52 HRS

The Emergency Department was already busy but Dr Scobie wasn't hard to find. Between treating a pub league footballer for a twisted ankle and a DIY enthusiast with a gashed hand, Holly caught up with him and took out the forms she needed filling in.

Scobie seemed a bit less offhand than the last time they'd met – perhaps because of Sergeant Stafford's "reminder" about good communications. Whatever the reason, Holly took the opportunity to ask him about Ashleigh while he scrawled on the paperwork.

"When someone's been knocked down like that, is it normal for them to be unconscious this long?"

"There isn't really any 'normal'," Scobie said without looking up. "I haven't seen her notes since she went upstairs, but I'd probably be expecting her to come round within the next twenty-four hours unless there's been major damage."

He signed the last form and handed it back to her. "How did the investigation go – did the rape kit show anything?"

Holly hesitated, but given that he seemed better disposed now she said: "She'd had unprotected sex but it's not clear whether it was rape."

Scobie nodded. "Well, at least she won't be pregnant."

"Sorry? I mean, how do you know?"

"If there's a suspected rape we ask whether the patient's using oral contraceptive. If not, we can suggest the morning-after pill to be on the safe side. Obviously I couldn't ask Ashleigh, but when I examined her arm I saw she'd a contraceptive implant." He gave her a significant look. "I'm only telling you that on the basis of good communications. You know what I mean?"

"Yes. Thanks, doctor."

"Yeah, well, thank your sergeant," Scobie said dryly. And with that he moved off towards the bay where the DIY man was bleeding.

Holly put the signed papers away and headed off along the corridor which led to the main entrance of the hospital. She wasn't really paying attention, though. Instead, her mind was running around the piece of information Dr Scobie had casually dropped out: Ashleigh Jarvis was using contraception.

It should have – would have – been no big deal, except for one thing: *She isn't like that. I mean she's not into boys yet – not serious: not more than fancying someone in a band or whatever, you know?*

That was what Lauren Booth, Ashleigh's best friend, had said. And Taz Powell had intimated the same thing: Ashleigh was still young for her age, not very mature.

So why have a contraceptive implant?

Of course, there could have been medical reasons, but somehow Holly was pretty sure that wasn't the answer. The more she thought about it, the more she believed that Ashleigh was a girl with secrets. The question was whether those secrets related to anything that had happened to her on Friday night. Or was it simply that Ashleigh Jarvis thought and did things that she would never admit – not even to her mother or her best friend?

4

Even though it was still well before opening time there were three cars parked on the rough patch of ground next to the pub and Drew Alford recognised one of them as Tommy Vickers's Merc. The man in the leather coat who stood beside it wasn't Vickers though, and as Alford made his way towards the side door of the red-brick building he knew he was being watched all the way.

The sensation only added to his suspicion that something had changed. It had struck him the moment he'd answered the phone twenty minutes ago and heard Tommy Vickers's voice say, "The Fox and Garter, Wellbeck Street. I want to talk to you."

"When?" Alford asked. He'd still been in bed and half asleep.

"Now," Vickers said. "Come in the side." Then the connection went dead.

That was when Alford knew that whatever the reason for being summoned, he'd better have his wits about him when he arrived.

There were several crates of empty bottles beside the side door and a couple of torn bin bags. For a moment Alford hesitated, then twisted the door handle and pushed it open.

Inside it was gloomy. There was a short corridor passing

the toilets, then an inner door with square glass panes. When Alford opened this he stepped into the pub lounge, with a dozen tables and closed curtains at the windows. Grey light came from a few wall lamps and the ceiling lights behind the bar.

A second man – older than the one outside but just as much a minder – was sitting at a table with a cigarette burning in an ashtray and a Sunday newspaper spread in front of him. He looked up as Alford came into the room. "Who're you?" he said, taking his cigarette from the ashtray.

"Drew Alford," Alford said. "Tommy called me."

The man looked him over for a second, then nodded and stood up. "Wait there." He moved off towards a door by the bar, disappearing through it.

Alford waited a moment. He could hear voices and an occasional bark of laughter from the other side of the pub – the saloon bar – but what was being said was too indistinct to make out. It sounded like there were several people in there, but even when he moved closer to the bar he couldn't see anything of the other room and after a moment he went back to where he'd been told to wait.

A minute or so later the door by the bar opened again and the man with the cigarette came back.

"He'll be here," he said.

Alford gestured towards the door. "What's going on?"

The man looked at him. "Poker," he said simply, then sat down and returned to his newspaper.

There was another burst of laughter mixed with a couple of catcalls from the other bar and a few seconds later Tommy Vickers pushed the dividing door open. He was dressed in jeans and an open-neck shirt, the sleeves pushed up his arms. From his expression it was impossible to tell if he'd won or lost on the last hand.

"What were you doing yesterday?" Vickers said without preamble, crossing the square-patterned carpet to where Alford was standing.

"Yesterday?" Alford frowned, as if the question didn't seem to have an obvious answer.

"The police," Vickers said. "They took you in. Why?"

"Oh, yeah," Alford said, making out that he finally understood. "It's okay, it wasn't anything to do with—"

"I didn't ask you that," Vickers cut him off. "I said *why*?"

Alford took it and nodded. "There was a girl, Friday night. She was attacked or some shit. I'd seen her – before it happened – and one of her mates tried to make out it was me."

"Was it?"

"No. No way."

Vickers eyed him suspiciously but Alford held his ground.

"It couldn't've been, could it?" he said. "You know where I was when it happened – the minimart, yeah?" He glanced at the guy reading the newspaper, as if he wasn't sure whether he should say more in front of anyone else.

"So what *did* you tell them?" Vickers said.

"Nothing. I mean, I told 'em I was over the other side of the estate with some mates. I knew they'd back me up. Got to, cos they were the ones with me at the minimart."

"The police say anything about that – the shop?"

"Nah, not a thing," Alford said. "Just this girl. Then they let me go. It's just coppers, yeah? Load of bollocks."

For a moment Vickers still looked distrustful, but then he shifted and Alford knew he'd sold the lie.

"As long as it is," Vickers said, then he dismissed the subject. "Okay, I've got something else for you. Cloudsley House, that's your patch, right?"

Alford thought about it quickly. Cloudsley House wasn't his turf because there'd never been any reason to claim it. Now though...

"Sure," he said. "It's ours."

"So no one's gonna give you a problem if you come and go?"

"Not if they've got any sense."

Vickers nodded, as if that was the correct answer. He put his hand in his pocket and took out a key ring with two keys hanging from it.

"Flat 407. It's empty – least, it's supposed to be. I need someone to keep an eye on it – go up once a day and make sure it's secure: no one hanging around."

"I can do that," Alford said. "No sweat."

"Hold on, I haven't finished yet. – Time to time you'll

get a call from Malc." He gestured to the man with the newspaper. "That's Malc. When he tells you, you go up and wait inside the place till someone comes, then you let them in. Either they'll be leaving something or taking something. Whichever it is, you wait till they've finished then lock up behind them. The rest of the time, stay away – you don't use it for a shag pad or parties, nothing like that, and it's only you who goes in there, understood?"

"Yeah, got it," Alford said. "What's the stuff gonna be?"

Vickers shook his head. "You don't need to worry about that. You're just the caretaker, right? You get fifty a week, maybe a bit more, depending. Main thing is, you don't attract attention. You keep everything nice and quiet so no one asks questions."

"Okay," Alford said. "No problem."

Vickers gave him a look, then tossed him the keys. "Start today – check it out and make sure it's okay. Any problems, call Malc."

"Okay."

"And remember, anything goes missing that shouldn't, I'll know who to look for."

Alford looked pained. "I know that," he said. "I'm not stupid."

"I know," Vickers said. "That's why you're here."

And with that he turned and headed back towards the other bar.

Alford pushed the key ring deep into his jeans pocket.

As he did so he became aware that the man called Malc was watching him. The man beckoned him over.

"All right?" Alford said, careful to keep it neutral – not too matey. He reckoned a guy like Malc would want some respect, because he looked pretty hard, although he had that flabby-round-the-chin look, like Alford's dad.

Malc said nothing, but shifted his weight and pulled a wad of notes from his pocket. He peeled off two twenties and a ten.

"This week's up front," he said as he handed the notes to Alford. Then he tore a thin strip from the top of his newspaper and wrote a number on it.

"That's me," he said. "You don't call Tommy even if something's wrong – '*specially* if something's wrong. Got it?"

Alford nodded.

"Okay, go on then, fuck off. I'll talk to you later."

5.

ITU
QUEEN VICTORIA HOSPITAL
09:57 HRS

In the Intensive Therapy Unit Dee Jarvis was reading aloud to her daughter from a magazine. Mrs Jarvis looked a little less drawn than the last time Holly had seen her, while Ashleigh remained worryingly pale, with a breathing tube still in place and a surgical dressing on the side of her head. She also looked younger than she was, perhaps because of the teddy bear-patterned nightdress she was wearing. Holly knew it as the sort of thing your mum would choose from your drawer because it still fitted, even though you'd stopped wearing it ages ago.

Holly knocked on the open door and paused just outside. "Mrs Jarvis? I'm TPO Blades from Morningstar Road police station. I came in with Ashleigh from the scene – from the accident on Friday."

"Oh. Oh, yes," Dee Jarvis said, standing up. "Sorry. There was so much going on then… I lost track of everyone's names."

She came over to Holly, the magazine still in her hand.

"That's okay," Holly said. "How is she?"

"They think she's a bit better," Dee Jarvis said. "They say the swelling is going down – you know, in her brain. They say that's good. And she's breathing without a machine since yesterday, but she still hasn't woken up. They don't really know how long that might take, but it could be any time."

Holly nodded in what she hoped was a positive way. She felt slightly awkward discussing Ashleigh while she lay there, even though she was unconscious.

"I hope it's soon," she said. "I came in to bring you Ashleigh's bag back. You just need to check the contents and sign a receipt."

"Oh, right, yes. Thank you," Dee said.

The only table in the room was crowded with cards and flowers, so they went outside to a couple of chairs. Dee Jarvis sat down on one and used the other to go through the bag, checking its contents against the list on the evidence form.

Holly waited a moment, then put on a tone of voice that she hoped sounded casual enough to mask the lie she had worked out.

"There was one thing I was asked to check," she said. "At the scene they found a packet of contraceptive pills near the bag. They wondered if they could be Ashleigh's."

Dee Jarvis looked up. "The pill? No, they're not Ash's."

"You're sure?"

"She's only fourteen," Dee said, leaving no room for doubt. "We've talked about it – you know, the whole thing – but she's still too young for all that yet. Even if she had a boyfriend... When she does, well, that'll be different, but she knows how I feel about – about getting in too deep before you're ready.

That was what happened to me."

"You were a young mum?" Holly asked.

"Not so young – eighteen – but I was involved too soon. The wrong bloke, like everyone told me, except I wouldn't listen."

Holly nodded. She was uncomfortable to have been told so much because of her lie, but at least it proved that her hunch was right. She still wasn't sure what it added up to, but when she saw Dee take Ashleigh's mobile out of the bag Holly found herself speaking before she'd really thought it through.

"Could I look at that for a moment?" she asked, extending a hand.

"Sure," Dee passed the phone across. "The battery's probably flat though."

The phone was a Nokia with a touch screen, not dissimilar to Holly's own. She pressed the power button and immediately the screen lit up, but wanted a PIN. Dee Jarvis shook her head when Holly asked if she knew it.

"More than my life's worth to look at her phone," she said, raising a smile. "Bet you're the same."

Holly nodded, smiled back, but then put on a serious tone. "I think there might have been a mistake," she said. "If the phone's locked it could mean no one's examined it – I mean, Forensics. Would it be all right if I took it back to the station just to be sure?"

"Well, I suppose…" Dee said, but she sounded uncertain.

"I'll make sure you get it back right away," Holly said. "I just don't want to get the blame if they *should* have held on to it."

"No, you take it," Dee said, making up her mind. "Ash doesn't—" She caught herself, seemed to shiver slightly, then made an effort. "As long as she can have it back when she wakes up."

"I'll make sure," Holly said.

Ashleigh's mother forced another smile. "I trust you," she said.

6.

INCIDENT ROOM
MORNINGSTAR RD STATION
10:24 HRS

Ashleigh's phone didn't really weigh the same as a brick in her pocket, but it seemed to, and Holly knew there were a ton more waiting to fall on her. Ever since she'd left the hospital she'd had a growing feeling that she had stepped over a line and now there was no going back. The only way out was to finish what she'd started, so when she re-entered the station she headed for the Incident Room instead of Custody.

As she'd expected, the place was unoccupied, the lights off, door locked. For a moment she hesitated. This was probably the stupidest thing she could do. She had no business and no authorisation to be in the room, but given that the case had been more or less dropped, and as long as she wasn't actually interfering with anything...

She made up her mind, keyed in the door code she'd memorised yesterday and let herself in.

The whiteboards were still as they'd left them the day before and Holly stood far enough back that she could see everything together: timelines, names, locations, evidence. But it was the photo of Drew Alford that took her attention most, and she realised that it was something about him that was bothering her. It was something to do with his interview, his version of events, but she couldn't quite pin it down. Was it something he'd said?

Holly crossed to a desk and located a DVD in a jewel case: the copy of the interview footage DS Woods had showed to DI Connors yesterday. She prised the disc out and took it to the DVD player, switching the TV on as it loaded.

She knew she didn't have time to watch the whole interview again, but as the screen came to life, Holly pressed *FFW* and let the picture run through at 8x speed. She was hoping that something would jog her memory even at that speed, but except for the small, jerky movements of Alford's head as he was questioned, very little else changed. He kept the same posture, sitting back in his seat, arms folded, legs crossed, resistant and defensive. You could just see he was denying everything.

Then, about three or four minutes before the interview was terminated, something changed. Suddenly, because of the playback speed, Alford seemed to jerk into a different position. His legs were uncrossed and he sat forward, arms on the table.

Holly pressed *pause*, then rewound the disc to the point where Alford changed position. When she pressed *play*, Alford was speaking:

"*...So she says, 'I'm a ten. You want me to show you?' And I said sure. So she says, 'Let's go over there where it's private,' and we go over to the bin shelter. That's where she starts snogging me, right? I'm telling you, she's the one doing it all –*

snogging me, rubbing up, right? You know what I mean. She says she's fancied me for ages but didn't want no one to know."

And that was it, Holly realised, stopping the disc. Everything he'd said before that point in the interview had been distrustful and defiant. But here he was speaking without being prompted and his body language was open and candid. *That* was the difference – and however much she might not like or trust Drew Alford, if Holly had to say how she interpreted what he was saying at that point, she would have to say "true".

So what did it all mean? How did it fit together?

She says, "I'm a ten. You want me to show you?"

That wasn't the Ashleigh her mother and best friend knew – the girl who wasn't interested in boys yet and was young for her age. No, that was a different Ashleigh: one who'd had unprotected sex sometime on Thursday or Friday, had given Drew Alford the come-on, and who'd had a contraceptive implant without telling her mother.

There were *two* Ashleighs, Holly was certain of that now – and the more she thought about it, the more she began to suspect what might really have happened to her on Friday night.

7.

CID
MORNINGSTAR RD STATION
10:42 HRS

Unlike the round-the-clock rota for uniform officers, CID generally only worked nine to five on weekdays. Unless there was a major investigation in progress, nights and weekends were covered by a single CID Duty Officer and today that was Danny Simmons, which was good – or at least, Holly hoped it would be.

He had three empty takeaway coffee cups on his desk and was typing – badly – at a computer terminal when Holly walked in. The rest of the office was empty and quiet.

"I think I might be in trouble," Holly told him when he finally looked up from the notes he was transcribing.

"Why, what've you done?" The way he said it made it clear that he thought there was a punchline coming.

"I've got Ashleigh Jarvis's phone," Holly said, taking it out of her pocket. "I didn't— I took Ashleigh's bag back to her mum and when I saw the phone I asked if I could bring it back here. I didn't tell her the truth about why I wanted it, though."

Seeing the phone, Danny Simmons leaned back in his chair, realising now that this wasn't a bit of banter. "It's been checked out of evidence?"

Holly nodded. "All the stuff in her bag has."

"So why do you want it?"

"I don't think anyone's looked at it. I mean, not at what's on it. It's still locked, so…"

"There wasn't any need to send it for technical analysis," Danny said. "It can't give us anything we don't already know."

"Do you think you *could* get it looked at?"

"Why?"

Holly took a moment, then glanced round and moved to an empty whiteboard. She picked up a marker pen. "Just let me go through it, then you can say it's crap and I'll go away, okay?"

"Fair enough," Danny said. He stood up from his desk and came round to watch as Holly drew a horizontal line on the board, then crossed it at four different points along its length.

"18:00 hours, Ashleigh leaves Lauren's house… 18:40, she texts her mum: '*Home soon*'… 18:45 approximately, she meets Drew Alford and they go to the bin shelter… 19:05, she runs away from Alford and into the road and gets knocked down." Holly looked to the DC. "Yes?"

"Yeah, but we know all this."

"I know, but this is what doesn't make sense: she leaves Lauren's house at 18:00 and says she's going home, then she texts her mum at 18:40 like she's only just leaving Lauren's."

Holly turned to the diagram and drew a wavy line between the two points in time.

"So what was she doing between 18:00 and 18:40?"

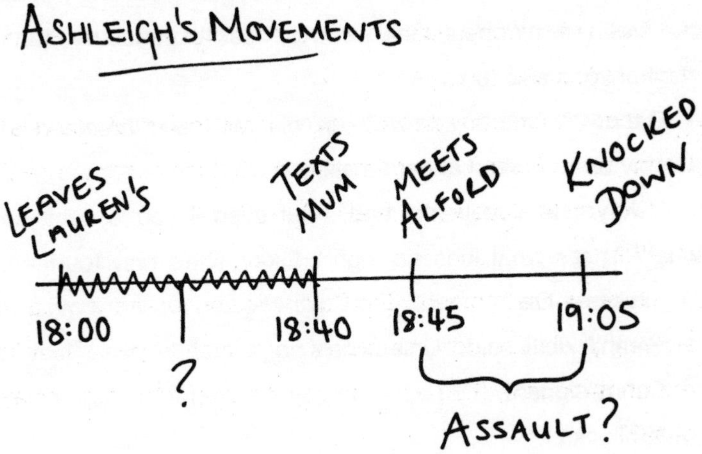

ASHLEIGH'S MOVEMENTS

LEAVES LAUREN'S
TEXTS MUM
MEETS ALFORD
KNOCKED DOWN
18:00
?
18:40
18:45
19:05
ASSAULT?

Danny Simmons studied the diagram, then made to speak, but Holly said, "Hang on. There are two other things: first, Ashleigh's got a contraceptive implant but her mum doesn't know. Second, she'd had unprotected sex with someone on Thursday or Friday, but everyone who knows her says she doesn't even have a boyfriend."

"Maybe she didn't want anyone to know."

"Yeah, it was a secret," Holly said. "But that's the point, isn't it? *Why?* Most girls can't wait to tell their mates about the lad they're going out with, but Ashleigh didn't even tell Lauren, her best friend. When I asked Lauren if Ashleigh had a boyfriend she said no. Everyone says Ashleigh isn't that kind of girl. But I think they've got it wrong. I think she *is* that kind of girl. I think she's seeing someone and that she's having regular sex with him."

She tapped the space between 18:00 and 18:40. "I think she was with him here. She went to meet him and she didn't want anyone else to know."

Danny Simmons screwed up his face and breathed in audibly as he looked at her timeline.

"Okay," he said in the end. "But even if you're right, so what? That's what kids do, right? Okay, she's only fourteen, but unless– Oh."

"Yeah," Holly said. "Unless he's *not* a kid."

Danny sighed.

"Bollocks."

"I can't see any other way to explain it," Holly said. "I think the reason it's such a big secret is that he's older – maybe quite a bit – which means he's been committing an offence by having sex with her."

Again, Danny sighed. "You came up with this on your own?"

Holly nodded. "There's something else too. I think Drew Alford was telling the truth when he said Ashleigh gave him the come-on. I don't know why she would or what that's got to do with the secret boyfriend, but..."

"Let's just stick to the mystery boyfriend," Danny said. "You're thinking if we can get into Ashleigh's phone we might find out who he is, right?"

"Yes. He's bound to have called her, so if we trace the number..."

Danny shook his head. "I can't send the phone down to Technical. It costs us to get things examined and I can't authorise it. DS Woods or the DI would have to decide if they had the budget."

"But if it gets us an answer...?"

"And if it turns out to be some spotty fourteen-year-old boy she was just too embarrassed to talk about..."

"Do you think it is?"

Danny didn't answer immediately, then for the first time he sounded irritable. "You couldn't have waited till bloody Monday, could you?"

"I'm off tomorrow."

"That's what I meant."

Holly couldn't tell how much – or even *if* – this was supposed to be taken as a joke. She took a beat, then she said: "What if we could unlock the phone and look at it without having to get anyone else involved?"

"How'd we do that?"

"Hold on," Holly said and took her own mobile out of her pocket.

8

As he strode up the hill towards the edge of the estate Drew Alford fingered the keys in his pocket and thought about the flat in Cloudsley House. For a moment he wondered if he should have been less definite when he'd claimed it was Kaddy Boys turf, but he didn't harbour the doubt for long. Tommy Vickers was only interested in getting what he needed and Alford knew that if he'd shown any doubt, Vickers would have found someone else for the caretaking job.

Not that the job in itself was such a big deal. Alford was already making the same money and more from leaning on the estate shops and street dealers who wanted to sell on the Cadogan. No, it was what this new job represented that made it important: he wanted the in with Tommy Vickers, and to get it he knew you had to do the small stuff first; to prove you could deliver and work your way up.

Of course, none of the others was bright enough to realise that, but that didn't matter. They'd do what he told them and that was enough. It was just a pity Vickers hadn't chosen a flat in one of the blocks where Alford or one of the other Kaddys already had a claim. Still, if it had to be Cloudsley, the only person he'd have to bargain with – or put down – was Ry Atkins. There was no one else who could give him a problem.

At the top of the road Alford was about to turn towards the looming grey block of Penrice House when a sharp whistle cut the air. He looked for its source and saw Ryan Atkins standing with his mates at a corner – it was as if thinking about him had made him appear.

Ryan didn't move. He watched Alford half hesitate, then continue his walk up the slope towards them. When Alford took his hand from his pocket Ryan was quick to check it out, but the hand was empty, as if Alford had been making a point.

"Stay here," Ryan said without turning his head to look at Dav, Tree or Simm. As he started forward he felt the pressure of a tightly compressed ball of determination in his chest.

He strode towards Alford and when he was two or three paces away he said, "I've been looking for you." His tone was flat and uncompromising.

"Yeah? What about?" Alford took one more stride and stopped, flicking a quick glance towards Dav and the others. Despite being outnumbered he showed no sign of concern.

"My old man's car," Ryan said. "Someone chucked a can of paint over it and sprayed your tag on the bonnet."

Alford shook his head. "Don't know nothing about it."

"So how come it's your tag?"

Alford shook his head again. "Wasn't me. Why would I?"

"Cos you're a twat."

Alford stiffened and Ryan's hands twitched involuntarily,

expecting a sudden rush towards him. And in some ways that was what Ryan wanted because it would confirm what he already knew: that Alford was guilty and needed to be put down.

But instead of losing his temper Alford shook his head for a third time. "Not me," he said, addressing both accusations. "I'm telling you. I wouldn't even know what car's yours."

Ryan watched him carefully. There was something about the way Alford stood now – straightforward and upfront – that made Ryan wonder if he'd got it wrong. Despite his previous certainty he knew that if Alford *had* done the car he wasn't the type to deny it. More likely to challenge and be done, even if he was alone and in the open.

As if sensing Ryan's hesitation Alford shifted and gestured towards the estate. "Listen, I wanted to talk to you anyway," he said. "I've got something – a deal, if you want it."

"What sort of deal?"

"Your lot and mine, going in together."

"Huh," Ryan said dismissively. "Why'd we do that?"

"Cos," Alford said. "You know Madder, right? He reckons he could knock out twice what he does now if he sells in your block."

"I ain't stopping him."

"Yeah, you are. He's not gonna go in there if he thinks you'll do him over. But if you're in with us he knows he can come and go. He makes more money, we take more for our cut, everyone's happy. Plus there's the other stuff. We divvy it all up. You don't need to do much if you don't want to."

"If we don't need to do anything, why'd you cut us in?"

Alford nodded, as if this was a fair point. "You'd have to do something," he said. "But that's not what it's about – listen, I don't care about them—" He gestured to Dav and the others. "It's you, yeah? You're the same as me."

"Yeah, right."

"No, listen. I mean you know what's what, right? You don't take any shit. So I'm saying, if it was you and me working together 'stead of separate…"

He let the sentence tail off, as if the possibilities were endless, but Ryan was still suspicious.

"So you give me a split just for hanging out?"

"I'm saying, there's stuff we could do, money we could make, if we're running this fucking place between us. I've got contacts, okay? That's all I'm saying. No bullshit. And if we've gotta live on this bleeding estate we might as well get something out of it, right? – Think about it."

He held Ryan's eye for a beat longer, then without waiting for a reply he turned and resumed his stride towards the tower of Penrice House.

Ryan didn't try and stop him. He watched Alford until he was a few metres away and then he moved back towards Dav and the others.

"So what's he say?" Simmo wanted to know as Ryan nodded for them all to move on.

"Reckons it wasn't him."

"Fuck off, that's bollocks. It's his fucking tag."

"Yeah, maybe," Ryan said. He looked up at the ugly concrete blocks that surrounded them and tried to figure out if Drew Alford had really meant what he'd said. And despite his instinctive suspicion, Ryan couldn't help thinking he just might have been telling the truth.

9.

INCIDENT ROOM
MORNINGSTAR RD STATION
11:03 HRS

"Just don't ask," Danny Simmons said when Oz Sitwell gave him a dubious look. At the desk Sam was taking the back off Ashleigh's phone and removing the battery.

It hadn't been Holly's plan for Oz to become involved when she'd called Sam and asked him to come to the Incident Room. But Oz had arrived with him and he was clearly intrigued as much as he was wary that this was all a bit dodgy.

On the other hand Sam seemed to like the fact that his skills were being sought. He peered inside the phone's battery compartment to read the serial number, then turned to the computer and typed the string of figures into the waiting box on the website he'd found. He hit enter, and after a brief wait the screen changed, displaying a ten-digit code. When he saw it Sam replaced the battery in the phone and switched it on. A few seconds later the start-up screen appeared and Sam keyed in the code from the website.

"Is that it?" Holly asked. As she said it the phone played the welcome chime.

"Yep, got it," Sam said with satisfaction.

"You sure you haven't wiped it or anything?" Danny

Simmons asked, concerned.

"No, it's fine. I just reset the PIN. It's not protected any more but nothing else has changed."

He picked up the phone and then hesitated, unsure who to give it to.

Danny Simmons took it. "Thanks," he said.

"I haven't seen any of this," Oz told Danny. "But Hol's supposed to be in Custody and Staff's going to wonder where she is."

Danny nodded. "I'll sort it. Ten minutes."

Oz still looked doubtful but he was distracted by a call on his PR: "*Three-One-Seven from Delta Mike, receiving?*"

"Three-One-Seven, go ahead."

"*Report of criminal damage, Cadogan Estate. Free to deal?*"

Oz gestured to Sam. "Come on, Bill Gates. Play time's over." Then into his radio: "Yes yes."

"Thanks," Holly said to Sam as he made to follow Oz out of the room.

He grinned. "You owe me," he said.

Danny Simmons was now leaning on a desk, scrolling through the address book on Ashleigh's phone. Holly moved to look over his shoulder. It was immediately obvious that there were fewer contacts listed than she would have expected. Perhaps twenty in all.

"How many people have you got on your phone?" Danny asked.

"Dunno, I've lost count." That was true. What was also true – although she didn't say so – was that since she'd joined the TPO scheme she hardly spoke to any of them any more.

"More than this, though," Danny said.

Holly nodded. "Yeah, but from what Lauren and Taz said, Ashleigh doesn't have a lot of mates."

"Might make it easier to spot the boyfriend on the list then."

"There's a quicker way than that. Have a look at the call log."

"Here." He handed her the phone. "I need more coffee for this."

He moved off to the machine in the corner and Holly looked at the phone for a moment, then dropped out of the address book and went to the call history – made and received.

The last name was *Mum* – an outgoing call; then *Lauren* twice – one incoming, one outgoing; then *Bic* – incoming; *Lauren*; *Shaz*; *Bic*; *Lauren*; *Bic*...

After running down the list Holly skipped out of it and into the text folder. There were half a dozen threads under different names, but one stood out with more than 250 items.

Holly looked up. "He's called Bic," she called across the room.

"How do you know?" Danny picked up his coffee and headed back.

"Look – no one else has sent her so many texts, or if they have she hasn't kept them."

She held the phone so he could see the screen. He looked

for a moment, then sighed as if he'd just been told he had a week of night duty coming up.

"Okay," he said. "I'll ask Sergeant Stafford if he can spare you."

10.

CLOUDSLEY HOUSE
CADOGAN ESTATE
11:24 HRS

"Looks like they chucked it from here," Oz said, miming a throwing motion towards the paint-covered Fiesta.

"It says it's gloss on the tin," Sam said, holding the paint can up by the handle and keeping it well away from his uniform.

"No chance of getting it off then, not without sanding it back. Probably cost more than the car's worth."

"What about the tag?" Sam asked, lowering the paint can carefully into the evidence bag.

Oz nodded and moved round to look at it again. "Yeah," he said. "No prizes for that."

Sam glanced away to where Leyton Atkins was talking to a couple of men who'd come out of the ground-floor flats to watch the proceedings. His smart Sunday suit, and that of his younger son, Charlie, set him apart from the other men's jeans and sweatshirts.

"Do you think it could be connected with Charlie getting assaulted yesterday?" Sam asked. "I mean, if that was Tyler Smith and he's one of the Kaddy Boys and that's their tag..."

Oz nodded. "I'd give you odds," he said. "Course, the one who'll really know is Ryan – not that he's going to tell us."

He gestured to where Ryan Atkins was watching them with three other youths. They were all keeping their distance.

"So what do we do?" Sam asked.

"Go through the motions," Oz said, then turned and called out: "Mr Atkins?"

Leyton Atkins looked over, then disengaged himself from the other men and crossed towards the two officers. Charlie followed him.

"Have you found anything?" Mr Atkins asked as he approached.

Oz shook his head regretfully. "At a guess I'd say it happened last night – probably late on when there was less chance of anyone seeing them."

"What about catching them? Can you get fingerprints or anything like that?"

"There might be something on the paint can," Oz said. "We'll take it in and see if Forensics can get something, but I wouldn't be too optimistic. The fact they dropped it here probably means they knew they hadn't left any prints."

He shifted a little and indicated the bonnet of the car. "Do you know about this tag – KB?"

"No, I don't know what it means," Mr Atkins said.

"Well, round here it usually stands for Kaddy Boys," Oz said. "They're a local gang and the tag's their way of marking territory."

"So if you know who they are…"

"You can't prove it from that, Dad," Ryan Atkins said. He'd

moved closer to hear what was being said. "Anyone can do a tag."

Oz nodded. "Ryan's right," he said. "But the thing is, to me it looks like they targeted your car in particular rather than any of the others. Do you know of any reason why they'd do that?"

"You mean why they'd pick on my car?" Mr Atkins asked. "No. There's no reason. I've always parked it here, for years."

"There's no reason they'd have a grudge against you?" Oz looked at Charlie. "What about the incident yesterday? Do you think this might be connected?"

"I— I don't know," Charlie said, glancing at Ryan.

"Ryan, what do you think? Do you know any of the Kaddy Boys?"

"Yeah, right," Ryan said. "I know them from church."

"Ryan..." his father started, but Ryan suddenly seemed to have had enough.

"Look, what's the point?" he said. "They're not gonna catch anyone. They're just going to fill in a few forms and forget it. It's a waste of time. The car was clapped-out anyway. I don't know why we've still got it."

"Hey! You listen," Mr Atkins said, his voice hardening. "Me and your mother saved for more than a year to buy that car, God rest her. You think I earn enough to just go out and buy another one? You think I don't have enough expenses already? Where's your sense, boy?"

"Where's *yours*?" Ryan snapped back, and he spun on his heel and strode back to his mates.

Behind him Mr Atkins looked stunned, as if Ryan had never spoken back to him quite so forcefully before. But it was Charlie's reaction that caught Sam's attention. The younger boy's face showed both upset and worry, as if everything that had just happened had simply added to a heavy load already on his shoulders.

Sam glanced at Oz and saw that he, too, was watching the boy and might have been thinking the same thing. The PC didn't comment on it though – just handed Sam the incident forms.

"Okay, Mr Atkins," Oz said. "If you'll give TPO Marsden your details, then I'll give you an incident number so you can contact your insurers with a claim."

11.

INCIDENT ROOM
MORNINGSTAR RD STATION
11:43 HRS

"Bic's phone is a pay-as-you-go, first registered on October 23rd last year," Danny Simmons said, hanging up the phone. "No way to trace who bought it."

He moved across to where Holly was studying the texts on Ashleigh's phone.

"Listen to these," she said. "They're from him to Ashleigh: *U R beautiful... Babe, I love what we do. I want it to go on for ever... Can't wait to see you... I love you so much.*"

"He's a real poet," Danny said dryly.

"They're all pretty short, but a lot of hers to him are longer. Some of them are a bit – you know – explicit."

"Yeah? Well just don't read them out to me then." He sipped his coffee, then he said: "It doesn't prove anything though. Bic could still be a spotty fourteen year old."

"I don't think so," Holly said. "They don't sound right for a teenager. *Babe, I love what we do. I want it to go on for ever?* Nah... There might be a way to find out for sure though."

"If you mean tracking down his phone, it won't work – at least, not accurately enough – that's only in the movies."

"No. Look, here." She scrolled back through the texts.

"This was from Thursday. Bic sends Ashleigh a text: *Romsey Road? 6 o'clock*. And she replies *Yes!* – So if that's where they met maybe there's something on CCTV. We could check, couldn't we?"

"Or I could just go home," Danny said flatly.

12

"Who did the car?" Alford demanded. They were standing at the bottom of the steps to the walkway outside Penrice House.

"What car?" Tyler Smith said, but as soon as he saw the look that crossed Alford's face he knew that he wasn't going to get away with it – and that he'd probably made it worse by faking ignorance.

"You know what fucking car, you arsehole," Alford said. There was a tautness about him that even Tyler was wary of.

It wasn't that he was afraid of Drew, but even though he was heavier and stronger, it was no guarantee of anything if they really got down to it. All the Kaddy Boys knew that when Drew was wound up like this he was as unpredictable as he was vicious.

"Okay, so what?" Tyler said, unwilling to completely ignore the insult.

"Fucking idiot," Alford said. "If I wanted that doing I'd've told you – shit." He glanced away and made a noise of annoyance, then looked back. "Was it just you?"

"Yeah," Tyler said.

"Why, what you got against Ry Atkins?"

"Nothing."

"So what the fuck did you do it for then?"

Tyler hesitated for a moment but he knew there was no way to avoid this admission now.

"It's his brother, Choirboy. He was at the minimart Friday night."

"What, inside?"

Tyler shook his head. "Outside, when I did the windows."

"And he saw you." It wasn't a question, because Alford had the whole picture now. "You twat."

"Listen—" Tyler said, and he straightened his shoulders to show he'd taken enough.

Alford took no notice of the gesture though. Instead he took a step away, thought for a second, then turned back. "Stay away from him from now on," he said. "If he hasn't told the cops already he probably won't – not unless you push him again. So just leave it, all right?"

"Listen," Tyler started again. "If—"

"Leave it," Alford repeated harshly. "I'll sort it."

Then he caught a glimpse of two figures approaching along the walkway. "Oh fuck, what now?" he said.

Even as they reached the top of the damp concrete steps Taz knew this wasn't a good idea. She'd tried to persuade Bex not to go looking for Drew, but Bex wouldn't listen. She wanted to have it out with him and there was no dissuading her.

Now Taz saw Drew standing with Tyler and she could sense that this wasn't going to be good: Drew just had that look about him. But if Bex saw it she took no notice. Instead she quickened her pace, descending the steps fast, as if she suspected that Drew would walk away before she could reach him. But it was Tyler who moved off and Drew who stood watching the two girls come down to his level.

"You weren't gonna call me then?" Bex demanded as soon as she was close enough to be sure she had Drew's full attention.

"I was gonna call you when I was ready," Alford said. "I had things to do."

"What, like being arrested?"

"I wasn't nicked," he said. "And if you know what was happening you know why I didn't call you."

"Yeah? That was yesterday though, wasn't it? What about today? What about till *now*?" Bex demanded. "Or didn't you want to see me cos of *why* they nicked you?"

Taz could see that this didn't go down well with Drew. "What's that supposed to mean?" he said coldly.

"You know what it means. You know what they're saying? That you got nicked for raping Ash Jarvis."

"Yeah, well *they* don't know fuck all. And if they say any more they'll get a smack. If I'd done it you think I'd be here now? Even the cops know I didn't."

"So why'd they nick you at all? They must've had a reason."

"Listen, I don't need this," Drew said. "I've got things to do."

He made to move away, dismissing her, but Bex was too angry. She stepped forward and grabbed his arm.

"You fancied her, didn't you?" she insisted. "I know you did. So had you been with her? Had you?"

"Get off me, bitch." Drew shook his arm, hard, to throw off her grasp.

"Tell me!" Bex shouted at him.

"Okay, so what?" he snapped at her. "So I'd seen her – earlier. Happy now?"

Taz saw Bex flinch as if Drew had slapped her. Without looking at him she moved in to try and draw Bex away. "Come on, let's go," Taz said.

But Bex was rooted to the spot. "What did you do?" she said, her voice suddenly quiet.

"What do you think?" Drew Alford's look was scornful. "And don't think it was cos of me. She was the one who wanted it, just so you know."

"Come on," Taz said again. All she wanted to do was get out of there now. She put her arm through Bex's. "Let's just go, yeah?"

She managed to get Bex to move, stiff like a robot, and they took a couple of steps before Bex turned back abruptly. "You arsehole!" she shouted. "You bastard. I wish they had locked you up. You should be!"

Taz saw Drew's face darken and he took a step towards them, threatening. She pulled Bex's arm, urging her to move again, and finally she did.

Behind them Alford watched the two girls hurry away for a couple of seconds, then he took out a packet of cigarettes from his pocket, lighting up before he moved off.

13.

IBO
MORNINGSTAR RD STATION
12:07 HRS

Holly knew this was make-or-break. She could also sense that with each additional minute that passed, Danny Simmons's doubts were getting stronger. Since they'd come up to Integrated Borough Operations he'd had two calls – one about a burglary artifice, the other over an alleged credit card fraud – and by rights he should probably have started to look into them.

Instead though, he was standing with Holly in the large, open-plan office, looking at a monitor as a civvie operator called Clare tried to find a camera with a view of Romsey Road and footage from Thursday evening. The longer it went on without a result, the more uncomfortable Holly became.

Finally the woman called Clare said, "There you go. It's the west end of the road, but that's all there is."

On the screen Holly could see the frozen, grainy image of a road junction. The lights of the passing cars tended to burn out the detail in places and the height of the camera angle made it difficult to see the faces of pedestrians. Even so, she examined the scene carefully, looking for anyone who could have been Ashleigh Jarvis.

"This is 18:00?" Danny asked.

"18:01."

"Can you run it back ten minutes?"

The images went into reverse and the time code ran back to 17:50. Then it started forward, but the effect wasn't smooth because the camera only recorded one second out of every three, giving the whole thing a disjointed, jerky feel.

Despite this, Holly scanned all the people she could tell were female, walking along the pavements, going into or coming out of buildings, sometimes obscured by passing vehicles. None of them looked like Ashleigh.

Then Danny Simmons's phone rang again. He answered it, taking a couple of steps off to the side. Holly stayed focused on the monitor, but she knew that Romsey Road was long and there was nothing to say that Ashleigh had met Bic within sight of the camera.

Danny ended his call. "I need to go back to the office," he said. "If you want to keep looking for a bit…"

"Okay," Holly nodded, not wanting to look away in case he changed his mind. "I'll let you know if I find anything."

She sensed his hesitation about leaving her, but in the end he moved off.

Then: "Danny?"

Holly looked to the operator. "Can you pause it?"

As Danny came back Holly pointed at the screen. "There. At the bus shelter. That's her."

The figure – a girl for sure – had long dark hair and a dark coat, short skirt. She was half under the shelter of a bus stop, looking off down the road.

"You think?" Danny said. Then to Clare: "Let it run."

The footage went forward again, still jumpy, but because the girl was standing still she became a fixed point. A slight turn of her head between one frame and the next and Holly was certain. "That's Ashleigh," she said.

Then an estate car came into view, silverish in colour, its indicator light on as it pulled in at the bus stop. At the same time Ashleigh Jarvis had moved out of the bus shelter and across to the kerb. The car door opened. She got in. The car was still for a few moments, then indicated and pulled away again.

"Can you see an index?"

Clare the operator shook her head. "Burned out. It's the lights. The old cameras can't deal with the contrast."

"Can we get a copy of this," Danny said, "and a couple of prints?"

By the time they were back in CID the phone was ringing again.

"Bloody hell," Danny said impatiently. "Sunday's *supposed* to be a day of rest." He picked up the phone. "CID, DC Simmons – Yes, that's right – When? – Okay, thanks for letting us know – Yes. Thanks."

He hung up.

"The Vic," he said. "Ashleigh came round half an hour ago."

14.

HUCKNALL WARD
QUEEN VICTORIA HOSPITAL
13:26 HRS

"Hello, Ashleigh," Danny Simmons said. "My name's Danny. This is Holly. We're from Morningstar Road station."

Ashleigh Jarvis still looked pale. Her lips were dry and the side of her face was bruised – green and yellow.

"Holly's the one who came with you in the ambulance," Dee Jarvis said. She was sitting on the edge of the bed, stroking her daughter's arm.

"Thank you," Ashleigh said, managing a wan smile.

"It's just my job," Holly said. "Would it be all right if we asked you some questions about the accident?"

Ashleigh nodded. "I don't remember very much though," she said.

Danny Simmons moved a green plastic chair next to the bed and sat down.

"You might find it gets clearer as time goes on," he said. "But for the moment we'd just like to find out what you remember from before the accident. Do you remember being at Lauren's house for example?"

Ashleigh nodded again. "Yeah," she said. "We watched telly."

"Do you remember leaving or calling your mum to say you were on your way home?"

"I think so."

"Okay. Anything else? – Anything from just before the accident?"

Ashleigh frowned, concentrating, but Holly was looking at Dee Jarvis. When Danny had asked the question Dee had stopped stroking her daughter's arm and tensed, as if bracing herself for the reply.

"I don't know," Ashleigh said then. "It's all sort of fuzzy. I can't describe it. It's like… It's like there should be something there but there isn't. It just sort of goes grey. Do you know what I mean?"

Danny nodded. "That's okay. Like I said, you might remember more later, or you might not. Don't worry about it."

Dee Jarvis shifted. "Maybe we should all let you get some rest," she said to Ashleigh.

"I've been in a coma, Mum. How much more rest can you get? I'm fine."

Danny Simmons glanced at Holly – her cue.

"Ashleigh, you know you said you remembered ringing your mum to say you were coming home? Can you remember where you were when you called her?"

For the first time Ashleigh hesitated, but only for a second. "I dunno. Leaving Lauren's, I suppose."

"Right. Only the thing is, Lauren told us you left hers at six and you didn't call your mum till twenty to seven. We know that from your phone."

"I don't know," Ashleigh repeated. "Lauren must've got it wrong."

"You didn't go somewhere else after Lauren's?"

"No, I just walked home."

"Did you meet anyone?"

"No. Why?"

"It's just to make sure we've covered all the details," Danny Simmons said, playing it down.

"What about Bic?" Holly asked.

"What?" Ashleigh made a small start at the name. "Who?"

"Bic?" Holly asked again, leaving it open.

"No, I don't know— Oh, you mean Bec – Bex. No. I didn't see her."

Holly frowned. "I thought it was Bic," she said. "Never mind. What about Drew Alford? Did you see him?"

"No," Ashleigh said. "I don't think so." Then she raised a hand to her head and made a pained expression.

"Are you *sure* you're all right," her mum asked, looking concerned.

"I think I'm getting a headache," Ashleigh said. "Maybe I *should* have a rest."

Dee Jarvis looked at Danny, who took the hint and stood up. "Don't worry," he said. "I think we've got everything we need. Thanks for your help, Ashleigh. Just concentrate on getting better, okay?"

"I will. Thanks."

They left the room and, after a moment with Ashleigh, Dee followed them into the corridor.

"I don't understand what's going on," she said, keeping her voice down but clearly confused. "Yesterday your DS Woods said you didn't think it was a– That she hadn't been..."

"No, we don't now," Danny said, coming in quickly enough to save her from saying the word she was trying to avoid. "Like I said, we just needed to make sure we'd covered everything."

Dee Jarvis seemed relieved by that. "I know you've got to do your job," she said. "It's just... You know."

"I know," Danny said. "Hopefully we won't have to bother her any more."

"We will though, won't we?" Holly said, once they'd moved out of earshot along the corridor. "We know Ashleigh was lying – about Bic and about Alford."

"Yeah," Danny said. "But I can't do any more, not without getting the DS to okay it."

He looked at her. "You ready for that? Is that what you want to do?"

Holly took a beat, then nodded. "We've got to, haven't we?"

15

"He's just such a bastard," Bex said, sniffling and dragging her sleeve across her face to wipe away her tears. "Going with her after we've been together for three months. And it wasn't like…it wasn't like I wouldn't – you know – wouldn't *let* him."

"I know," Taz said as sympathetically as she could. This was about the third time Bex had gone over it all in the last half-hour and Taz was starting to think she was just using the situation as an excuse to be dramatic.

"And everyone knows," Bex went on. "Or they will by tomorrow at school. I can't stand it."

"Just ignore them," Taz said. "Anyway, if he's going to do stuff like that…" She let the sentence trail off in the hope that it wouldn't give Bex anything more to get upset about.

"I should've chucked him at Christmas. I knew I should," Bex said. "Everyone said so."

"I know," Taz said again. "But you know what he's like now. No one's going to think it's your fault."

"I should've known he fancied her. You could tell. I just— I just didn't want to believe it."

She pulled a crumpled tissue from her jacket pocket and blotted her eyes. "Has my mascara run?"

"Only a bit. It's okay."

Bex sniffed. "He's a bastard," she said again.

"You want to go home?" Taz said. She was cold from sitting on the edge of the empty flower bed in the precinct and if Bex had had enough of crying for a while it was a good time to suggest moving.

Bex shook her head. "I want a drink," she said, casting a look towards the precinct off-licence, its lights on and door open. "I want to get shit-faced."

"They won't serve you," Taz said.

"Yeah they will. It's Tariq on the till. He always serves me, long as there's no one else there. He doesn't want Drew coming in."

Bex was searching her purse in a determined way now, coming up with a collection of loose change. "How much money you got?"

"I dunno. Not a lot," Taz said. "Anyway, I don't want any."

"Why not?" Bex gave her a pleading look. "Come on. I hate feeling like this. I hate being in love with him. I just want to feel better."

Taz knew if she didn't go along with this Bex would take it as another personal injury, so – reluctantly – she took a two pound coin from her jeans and handed it over.

"That'll get us a bit," Bex said, straightening up. "Cider, yeah?"

"Yeah, sure, whatever," Taz said.

16.

INCIDENT ROOM
MORNINGSTAR RD STATION
14:03 HRS

Holly was alone in the Incident Room with DS Ray Woods. He was sitting in a swivel chair, wearing a polo shirt and jeans under his open fleece. The clothes didn't give a clue as to what he'd been doing on his Sunday afternoon off before Danny Simmons had called him in.

Woods was looking at the prints from the CCTV camera footage.

"No index so we can't trace it – well, we might if we can pick it up on another camera either before or after this one, but that's a lot of hours to put in." He lowered the photographs. "Why should we?"

"If he's driving a car—" Holly started.

"You don't know *who's* driving. You can't see. Could be anyone. What if Bic got his mum to drive him there to meet Ashleigh, then they all went to the pictures together?"

"Sarge—"

"Listen, even if you're right, even if this Bic is an adult and he knows Ashleigh's underage, even if he is having sex with her—"

"He is. He must be."

For a moment Holly thought she'd gone too far. Woods was still, then he frowned.

"Okay, just for the moment let's assume Ashleigh *is* in a sexual relationship with an adult male, and let's assume they both know he'd be in trouble if anyone found out. Do you think Ashleigh's going to admit it and tell us who he is?"

Holly thought about it – about the way Ashleigh had dodged her questions earlier, and about the texts she'd read. "No. She thinks she's in love with him."

"Right. So the only way to identify him is going to involve costs – either man-hours trawling through CCTV, or Technical trying to trace his phone – that's if Ashleigh doesn't warn him and he doesn't ditch it."

"Sarge—"

"Wait – but let's say that we *do* find out who he is – we've still got to have sufficient grounds to arrest him, and there's nothing: nothing to show they've had a sexual relationship."

"We've got his DNA – the semen. That would prove it, wouldn't it?"

"In theory, but first we'd need solid ground to arrest him. We haven't got that so we can't take his DNA to match against the semen sample."

"What about the texts then?"

"Do any of them specifically say *when we had sex yesterday*? or, *I want to have sex with you again*?"

"Not exactly, but I haven't read them all. There might be something..."

Woods shook his head.

"But if we don't do anything... She's not going to stop seeing him. Nothing's going to change – she thinks it's okay. She thinks they're in love."

"I know. So tomorrow I can put it to the DI – see if she's prepared to spend the department budget, whether she wants to put the manpower into it and what the CPS view is."

He put the photographs aside and stood up. And then Holly knew that this was as far as she could go. There wasn't anything else.

"Okay. Thanks, Sarge," she said. "Sorry you had to come in. I'll get back to Custody."

She started towards the door and had covered most of the distance before Woods said: "You want to know why?"

Holly stopped and turned back. "Why what?"

"Why I came in on my precious Sunday off?"

Holly wasn't sure what this meant, or what the correct answer should be. "Er, yes," she said.

"It's because you don't know the half of it," Woods said.

"I don't understand."

"I know. You don't know how bad it might be."

He paused, shifted slightly, then shoved a hand into his pocket. Holly could tell he was thinking something through so she said nothing, hoping this meant he wasn't quite ready to walk away, despite what he'd just said.

"You asked Ashleigh about Bic, right?" Woods said in the end.

"Yeah. She pretended she thought I meant Bex."

Again the DS gave it some thought.

"Do you know what grooming is?" he asked then.

Holly nodded. "When a man gradually builds up contact with an underage girl, getting her more and more involved so that in the end she'll have sex with him?"

"Not just girls, but yes – and it's not usually just one. A predatory paedophile can be in contact with several kids at the same time. So what worries me is what'll happen if Ashleigh makes contact with Bic in the next few hours and he finds out we're interested in him. If he does, the first thing he'll do is ditch his phone and try to cover any trace of his contact with her. He'll disappear, but we won't just lose him – we'll never know who else he's doing this to either."

"Could he do that – just disappear, I mean?"

"Depends how sophisticated he is. But there's a good chance he's lied to Ashleigh about where he lives, his real name, his job, everything. He could live fifty miles away and only come to the city to meet her."

Holly nodded, realising it was true. Then she thought of something. "I don't think he does though – I mean, I think he's local."

Woods frowned. "Why?"

"Because he usually calls her or sends texts every day, but there's nothing on her phone from him since Friday. No missed calls, no new texts after she was knocked down. So I think he knows what happened, *and* that she's in hospital."

Woods thought about it. "Maybe," he said.

Then Danny Simmons came in. From his expression it was clear he wasn't sure what to expect and he looked at Woods – a question.

"Have you still got Ashleigh's phone?" Woods asked him.

Danny nodded. "It's upstairs in my desk."

"You'd better get it then."

"What about waiting till tomorrow?" Holly said, uncertain.

Woods shook his head. "I don't think we can now. The cat's half out of the bag and if you're right about him being local it means we might have even less time before he tumbles. So let's work out how we're going to find him without tipping him off."

17.

STAINSBY WARD
QUEEN VICTORIA HOSPITAL
16:17 HRS

There was nothing else to do, just wait and try not to keep looking at the mobile which lay on the bedside cabinet, resolutely silent since Bic's final text.

In the last hour Holly had become familiar with every inch of the hospital room: a single, bare bed, a couple of chairs, a few pieces of equipment. Nothing to hold your interest for more than a few seconds. And the view from the window where Holly stood now was little better. It was of a grey, rain-wet car park and landscaped banks of muddy grass. A few people came and went, but even though she watched every man she saw Holly knew there was no way to tell if one of them was the man they were waiting for. He'd probably look so ordinary that no one would look twice at him – no one except Ashleigh.

Or perhaps not *only* Ashleigh if DS Woods was correct. And from the seriousness with which Ray Woods was treating this operation, Holly knew that he really did fear the worst – that the man called Bic might not only be abusing Ashleigh Jarvis's trust, but that of any number of others.

* * *

"They've cloned the SIM card," Danny Simmons had told them when he returned to the Incident Room from Forensics. Then he'd passed a rather battered-looking mobile to Woods. "Anything we send from that will look as if it's coming from Ashleigh's number."

"What about her real one?"

"Bagged and tagged in evidence. They copied all the data onto a CD. I called Mrs Jarvis at the hospital and said we'd be returning it tomorrow, just in case Ashleigh asks for it."

"Okay," Woods had said, then turned to Holly. "So now you're Ashleigh. You're lying in hospital, you've got your phone and your mum's just gone out for a cup of tea or something. What do you do?"

"Text Bic."

Woods nodded and picked up a pen. "So what are you going to say?"

And so it had started.

The first text had been the hardest because it had to look natural and gain Bic's attention without raising suspicion. They'd talked about it, changed it and revised it for nearly twenty minutes before everyone was happy. Then Holly had copied the message off the whiteboard and onto the phone and pressed *send*.

14:23
Babe I feel terrible. Let me know ur there. I need 2 know.
Everyones asking questions. A xx

And then the first wait, but only for a few minutes. In the meantime Woods had put in a call to the hospital and Holly had heard him bartering a favour with a nurse. By the time he'd done that the cloned phone had chimed.

14:28

R u ok? R u still in hospital? Im worried about u. xx

"I'll bet he's worried," Danny said dryly when Holly had finished reading the text aloud. "Worried about what she's saying."

"And he knows she's in hospital," Woods said. He looked to Holly. "Okay, so what's Ashleigh want to say now?"

"I think she'd want to sound cheerful," Holly said. "You know, pretend it's better than it is."

14:32

Lots of bruises. Doctors say I have to stay here 3 or 4 days. Got a room of my own tho! Wish u could come. U make me feel safe. xx

The next reply was faster, as if the man at the other end of the connection was giving it his full attention now.

14:34

Want to make u safe more than anything. Who is asking questions? xx

"Okay, we're going," Woods said. "We'll reply on the way."

14:44
Battery low. Mum gone home. No one coming this afternoon til 5. Im in room 7 Stainsby Ward. Please come if u can. Need to know what to say. Luv u xx

Holly had sent the last text from the back seat of Woods's car as they drove to the hospital. Ten minutes later a staff nurse showed them to the empty room at the end of a corridor on Stainsby Ward – a floor below Ashleigh's real room – and then the waiting had begun.

"He'll come or he won't," Woods had said in answer to Holly's unspoken question as they looked round the empty room. "No way to tell."

And now, an hour later, they were still waiting.

Looking out of the window and watching the afternoon sky getting darker, Holly thought about Ashleigh Jarvis in a room upstairs, oblivious to what was going on below her.

Holly knew it wouldn't be hard for Ashleigh to put on the make-up and clothes to pass for eighteen or nineteen: they all could. And Holly wasn't so perfect that she hadn't blagged her way into pubs and clubs that way herself. Not often, true, and not since she'd been accepted as a TPO, but enough that she understood the ripple of excitement at getting away with it and the addictiveness of being treated as an adult. When it happened the world looked different, and afterwards it was hard to go back to being your real age again.

Pretending to be Ashleigh – if only in texts – had felt strange and Holly had mixed feelings about it. She didn't doubt that Ashleigh was in love with Bic, but by setting out to find him Holly and the others were going to destroy that. Perhaps worse though – at least to Ashleigh – would be the fact that they had made her feel like a kid again, not the adult she wanted to be.

And maybe she wasn't so different to Ashleigh, Holly thought. After all, they both had their secrets, and every time she put on her uniform Holly was also pretending to be older and more worldly than she really was. She had just as much chance as Ashleigh of getting in over her head; just as much chance of being exposed for what she really was.

This last thought wasn't a comfortable one, but Holly found it hard to shift. So when Danny Simmons opened the door of the room with a Coke and a coffee in his hands Holly was glad of the distraction.

"Anything?" he asked, nodding at the phone.

Holly shook her head. "Where's the DS?"

"End of the corridor. He went to talk to the nurses."

Danny put the drinks down and looked at his watch. Holly didn't bother to ask what he thought. She knew there was still no way to tell whether this was going to work.

"Is it okay if I nip out for a couple of minutes?" she asked.

"Best not. Why?"

"Loo break – unless you've got a bed pan."

Danny made a play of patting his pockets. "Sorry, all out – okay, but don't hang about though."

"I won't."

18

Charlie liked Sundays. Usually. Even though he knew it was supposed to be boring and dull and always the same, it was the predictability of the routine that made it reassuring: Sunday-best clothes, then church, then a roast lunch. Later: ironing, homework, getting ready for the week ahead. Some TV in the evening, bath or a shower, then bed in good time. That was always how it went.

But not today. Lunch had been late, and then the atmosphere had been sullen and quiet because Ryan hadn't appeared like he was supposed to and that had annoyed their father. Then, after they'd eaten more or less in silence, Leyton Atkins had spent an hour on the phone trying to get the insurance company to provide him with the hire car he thought he was entitled to but which they said he wasn't. Without the car he'd have to take three different buses to get to work, and after recent lay-offs at the joinery factory, Charlie knew his dad was worried about being late and putting his job on the line.

Charlie was worried too – about what Tyler Smith would do next. And he was also angry with himself – for not having done something before, for not standing up to Tyler yesterday in the stairwell. What he *should* have done was tell him then: *Leave me alone or I go to the cops and say who was in the minimart.*

Charlie wished now that he'd told Ryan about all this last night when he'd had the chance. He hadn't because he didn't want to seem like a useless kid, but he'd have swallowed his pride and explained things to Ryan if he'd appeared for lunch. So when he didn't, Charlie knew there was no choice: he would have to do something himself, before it got worse.

"I'm just going down to the rec area," he told his father.

"Be back before it's dark," Mr Atkins said without looking up from the insurance paperwork. Not a request.

Charlie nodded. "Might be sooner. I'll see who's there."

"And don't get those jeans filthy."

"I won't," Charlie said.

He left the sitting room and slipped into the kitchen for a moment. When he came out he took his jacket from the peg, then went along the hall and twisted the door lock. "See you later," he called, and he was gone.

19.

STAINSBY WARD
QUEEN VICTORIA HOSPITAL
16:22 HRS

As Holly emerged from the toilet she almost walked into Lauren Booth. The girl was carrying a coat over her arm and a bunch of flowers in her hand. She was looking at the room numbers as she went along the corridor and perhaps for that reason she didn't immediately recognise Holly. When she did she seemed surprised.

"Oh, hiya," she said. "I was looking for Ash's room. Do you know where it is?"

"She's upstairs," Holly said. "Hucknall Ward."

"Oh. I thought it was Stainsby."

"No. Sorry."

"Oh, okay. I'll try up there then. Thanks."

Lauren turned and started back towards the lifts, just as Holly thought of something.

"Lauren, hang on a sec. Who told you that Ashleigh was here, on this floor?"

Lauren frowned. "How do you mean?"

"Did you call the hospital to find out which ward she was on?"

"No, it was my dad."

Holly glanced round. "Is he with you?"

Lauren shook her head. "He stayed in the car. Why?"

"Oh, no reason, just wondered. Say hi to Ashleigh for me."

"I will."

She waited until Lauren had gone back around the corner, then moved quickly to Room 7.

DS Woods was standing with his back to the window when she entered and Danny Simmons looked up from the chair.

"Find a bed pan?"

Holly ignored him and looked to Woods. "Sarge, the hospital's telling anyone who rings or comes in that Ashleigh can't have visitors at the moment, aren't they?"

"Yeah." Woods nodded. "Why?"

"I just saw Lauren Booth in the corridor. She was coming here to see Ashleigh."

"Here? This room?" Danny Simmons asked.

"Yeah. She said her dad had called to find out where Ashleigh was, but if the hospital's saying no visitors..." She didn't bother to finish the sentence. She could see Woods coming to the same conclusion that she had.

"Was he with her?" Woods asked.

"No. Lauren said he was waiting in the car."

Woods took out his radio. "Delta Mike from DS Woods. Vehicle check, please. Any vehicle with a registered keeper Colin Booth, 165 Escott Road."

"*Received. Standby.*"

Woods picked up the mobile from the bedside cabinet and

turned to Danny Simmons. "Stay here in case we're wrong," he said.

"*DS Woods from Delta Mike. Re your vehicle check: only one vehicle shown for that address. Registered keeper Colin Ian Booth. A silver Vauxhall Astra. Index Yankee Papa 54 Alpha Alpha Echo.*"

"Received. Thanks."

Holly scribbled the number down on the back of her hand with a biro and then she realised.

"Sarge – Colin Ian Booth – C.I.B. Backwards that's Bic."

Woods looked at her, then gestured to Danny. "Forget staying," he said. "Come on. Sharpish."

And he was heading for the door before Danny Simmons was out of the chair.

20

Taz knew that Bex was putting it on, swinging between tears and anger and making out that it was because of the cider. She'd drunk nearly two cans – her own and most of Taz's – but Taz knew Bex wasn't really drunk and she was tired of the pretence. All she wanted to do was go in out of the cold.

She'd finally managed to persuade Bex to go back to hers, but as they headed towards Cranham House Bex spotted Tyler Smith and Skank standing together looking morose. There was no sign of Drew, which was good, but instead of keeping away from the two boys, Bex changed direction towards them.

"They can tell Drew," she said when Taz protested. "They can bloody tell him I'm not seeing him no more. *I'm* dumping *him*."

When Skank saw them approaching he nudged Tyler. "Oi-oi. Reckon we've pulled," he said.

Tyler looked, but with no real interest. He was still stinging from Drew's earlier bollocking and he was in no mood for Skank's lame jokes, or a pair of stupid girls – especially when one of them was Drew's bird.

"All right, girls," Skank said with a leer. He moved forward to meet them. "What's up?"

* * *

At first Charlie wasn't sure that the figure at the back of the group *was* Tyler Smith. He was with another lad and a couple of girls and Charlie could only see his back. One of the girls was making exaggerated gestures and speaking loudly, laying down the law. It wasn't until the other lad saw Charlie and said something that Tyler looked round.

In that moment Charlie hesitated. When Tyler came away from the others and marched towards him, Charlie strengthened his determination to go through with this. He had the reassurance in his pocket to help quell the weightless sensation he felt in his stomach, but he could see that Tyler's expression was brooding and malevolent.

"What you want, Choirboy?" Tyler demanded. "Didn't you get enough?"

"I've had enough of you," Charlie said, barely knowing where the words came from. He stopped a couple of metres from Tyler. "That's why I'm here. Cos if you do anything like that again I'm going to the police. I'm going to tell them what I saw, at the shop."

Tyler took a moment, as if he was surprised that Charlie was answering back when he should have been running. "Do that and you're dead," he said.

Charlie refused to let himself move. He shook his head. "Just stay away," he said. "I— I mean it. You do anything again and I'm going to the cops."

Then, without waiting for a reply, he let himself turn

and start back the way he'd come. He wanted to hurry, but he made himself stay calm. Three paces, four…

"Oi, Choirboy!"

Charlie heard the shout but didn't react until he heard quickening steps coming after him. With the sound came a jump from his heart and the instinct to break into a run – but as soon as he felt it, something snapped.

It was part fear and part anger, but part of it was also the knowledge that he couldn't get away now and he'd have to finish what he'd started.

So he turned to face Tyler and as he did so his hand came out of his jacket pocket, fingers locked round the handle of the kitchen knife. It was no more than a second before Tyler was on him, and in that moment Charlie felt the odd, half resistant, half yielding sensation of the knife blade piercing through fabric and flesh.

Charlie let go of the knife, stepped back. Tyler didn't move. The black plastic handle of the knife was still sticking out of his sweatshirt and he was looking down at it, puzzled. Then he took hold of the knife and pulled it out.

As soon as he did so there was a red welling of blood which spread quickly downwards to his belt.

Charlie took another single step backwards, eyes widening. He caught his heel on a flagstone and started to stumble, but then turned the motion into a run, taking off as fast as he could go, feet barely touching the paving.

"Shit!" Skank said, looking at Tyler.

Tyler Smith said nothing. The colour was draining out of his face as he stared at the wound in his belly. It was only when Bex started to scream that Tyler seemed to realise that all this commotion was because of him, and then he decided he had better sit down. He was still holding the knife.

21.

QUEEN VICTORIA HOSPITAL CAR PARK
16:25 HRS

By the car park ticket machines Holly, Woods and Danny Simmons stopped running and looked out over the tarmacked area. Every parking space seemed to be taken for as far as Holly could see in the growing gloom of the late afternoon.

"He could be anywhere," she said.

"What about just covering the exit? Till he leaves?" Danny suggested. "There's only one way out."

Woods looked dubious. "Yeah, but if Lauren goes back and says she saw Holly... I'd rather nick him with a chance of finding the phone on him." He looked at his watch, then made a decision. "We'll split up, one row each. We've still got time."

So they separated, with Holly taking the nearest lane of parked cars. She walked briskly but steadily, scanning left and then right, ignoring any car that wasn't silver, checking the index numbers of any that were against the registration she'd biro'd on her hand.

22.

BRANWELL ROAD
16:26 HRS

In the patrol car Sam and Oz were following a dodgy-looking pickup truck with a broken brake light when the radio came to life.

"*Delta Mike Five from Delta Mike. Pedestrian precinct centre of the Cadogan Estate. Report of an assault, possible stabbing. Free to deal?*"

Sam looked at Oz. It was his decision.

"Okay," Oz said. "I can't get enough of the Kaddy today."

He touched the brake and checked the mirror for a U-turn. Sam pressed *call* on the radio as Oz went to blues and twos.

"Delta Mike from Five. Yes yes. On way."

"*Received, Five. Anonymous female informant. Ambulance service informed.*"

"All received," Sam said. And as the Volvo made the turn he felt the now familiar adrenalin rush kick in.

23

Drew Alford arrived at a run, his mobile still in his hand from when Skank had called him. Rizza was following on his heels.

"You see who it was?" Alford said, his glance taking in but ignoring Tyler, Taz and Bex, and everything else except Skank.

Skank nodded. "That black kid, Choirboy. Ry Atkins's brother. Ty went after him an' next thing he's been stabbed. The kid ran."

"Shit," Alford said. In the distance he could already hear the two-tone sound of a siren.

"Tell them to piss off," he told Rizza, gesturing to Taz and Bex who were standing a little way off. They had their arms round each other, watching Tyler. "They didn't see anything. They weren't here."

"Taz called the ambulance," Skank said.

"Never mind. Tell them," he repeated to Rizza, then started briskly towards Tyler.

"What d'you want me to say?" Skank said, hurrying to keep up.

"You were here but you don't know who did it," Alford said, rattling it off as the siren got closer: "It was a white guy, about eighteen. You never saw him before. Not from round here. Got it?"

"Okay."

Alford stopped and squatted next to Tyler. His face was grey and he looked up dumbly at Alford. He was pressing a hand to his belly and it was covered in blood.

"Ty? Listen to me," Alford said. "You've got to listen…"

Fifty metres away a police car came round the corner at speed and then braked sharply. Seconds later it had stopped and two police officers were opening the doors and heading towards them at a run. Drew Alford continued to speak urgently into Tyler Smith's ear.

24.

QUEEN VICTORIA HOSPITAL CAR PARK
16:28 HRS

As Holly neared the end of the second line of cars a van came along the row towards her and she stepped aside to let it pass. As she did so she caught sight of a figure in the front seat of a car about ten metres away.

It could have been nothing – anyone was entitled to sit and wait – but just to be sure Holly took a few steps until she could make out the colour of the car. Silver. She went closer, straining to make out the index in the growing gloom. YP5…

A movement – the pale shape of a face – caught her eye. And at that moment she knew he was looking at her. And at the same moment, the car's headlights came on, making it impossible for her to see the rest of the number plate. The engine started up and a second later the car pulled forward, making the turn out of the space.

More by instinct than anything else, Holly stepped forward, blocking the centre of the traffic lane. She held up her hand as she walked towards the car, hoping it was commanding enough to make the driver stop.

It worked. The car halted and Holly closed in on it, waiting until the last moment before stepping around the bonnet and moving quickly to the driver's window.

She glanced round but there was no sign of DS Woods or Danny Simmons. Then the driver's window opened a short way.

"Is something wrong?" the man inside said.

Holly bent to the window. "It's just a routine stop, sir." And then, as if surprised to see him: "It's Mr Booth isn't it? Lauren's dad."

Colin Booth looked up at her through the part-open window, recognition coming to his face.

"Oh. Yes, I remember you. Holly, right?"

Holly nodded. "I'm sorry to stop you," she said. "We're just doing a vehicle check. It won't take a minute." She raised her radio. "DS Woods from Seven-Six-Two, receiving?"

"A check on what?" Colin Booth said. "I need to go. I'm meeting Lauren."

"Could you just bear with me a second?"

She heard Woods's voice in her earpiece. "*Go ahead, Holly*."

"Sarge, second parking area, left-hand side. I've got a stop."

"*Understood. On way.*"

"I do need to go," Colin Booth said, and there was a note of urgency in his voice now. "I said I'd meet Lauren at the entrance. I don't want to be late."

He reached down and Holly saw him put the car into gear. She put her hand on the door pillar in the hope that it would dissuade him from moving.

"Could you tell me the registration number of the car?" Holly said, hoping to distract him.

"Yes, it's YP54 AAE. Look–"

"And are you the registered keeper?"

"Yes! Look— Look, I'm sorry I have to go," Booth said and Holly could hear a rising note of panic in his voice. "I can't— I have to go."

As he said it, the car started to move forward.

Holly moved with it, staying alongside the driver's window, keeping a hand on it.

"Mr Booth, stop! – Mr Booth!"

But it wasn't going to happen. She caught a glimpse of Booth's face, rigidly staring forward as he changed gear. The car picked up speed, forcing Holly to let go. She kept on running behind it though, and as the distance increased she reached for her radio. "DS Woods from Seven-Six-Two. He's heading for the exit. It is Booth."

Ahead of her Booth's car made a turn. Holly heard the skid of tyres on damp tarmac as the car disappeared from sight. Then, a moment later, there was the blare of a horn, almost instantly followed by the sound of a collision.

Pushing herself to go faster, Holly reached the end of the row and swung round the final car in time to see Danny Simmons sprinting in from the opposite direction. They were both heading for the point where two cars – Booth's and another – were shunted together in a lopsided T-shape.

Holly reached Booth's Astra first, slowing down at the last moment when it became clear that it couldn't go anywhere. She approached the driver's door but waited for Danny Simmons to get there too.

"Go on, then," he told her. "It's your collar."

Holly moved forward and looked in at the man in the driver's seat. He was still staring rigidly forwards. She knocked on the window. "Mr Booth, can you get out, please?"

There was no response and after a second Holly reached down to the handle and opened the door.

"Mr Booth?"

For a moment longer Booth sat immobile. Then his chin sagged to his chest and his shoulders started to shake. But it wasn't until he started to make an odd kind of choking sound that Holly realised he was crying.

25

"I didn't mean it. He just— He ran on to it."

Charlie was shaking and close to tears from the shock and the fear of what he had done.

"Okay," Ryan said, still holding his brother's arm. "You got any blood on you?"

"I don't know," Charlie said. He looked down at himself helplessly. "I don't know," he repeated.

Ryan stepped back to look him over, then took his brother's hands and checked them as well. "No, you're okay," he told him. "Where's the knife?"

"Back there. I— Tyler had it."

"Shit," Dav said, but Ryan shot him a look.

"Don't worry about that," Ryan told Charlie, trying to sound positive.

"But what if he dies?" Charlie said, finally voicing his worst fear.

"*He* came after *you*, right?" Ryan said firmly. "You were only defending yourself. But it's not gonna get to that, okay? It's gonna be fine."

He turned to Dav. "Take him home. I'll go and see what's happening."

"Can't you come?" Charlie said, unable to keep the pleading note out of his voice.

"Not yet," Ryan said. "I'll be there in a bit, okay? Just go home and pretend nothing's happened. Don't say anything. That's important. Nothing, okay?"

Charlie swallowed but made a tight nod.

"Go on then," Ryan said, and he gave Charlie's shoulder a squeeze. "It'll be okay."

26.

QUEEN VICTORIA HOSPITAL CAR PARK
16:33 HRS

"...But it may harm your defence if you do not mention when questioned something which you later rely on in court..."

"Dad? – Dad, what's happening? What's the matter?"

"Lauren, it's all right. It's just— It's just an accident – the car – that's all."

"...Anything you do say may be given in evidence."

"Can you stand back over here for me please, Lauren?"

"You understand the caution?"

"Yes."

"Okay. And because I have reason to believe you've committed an offence, we're going to carry out a search of your vehicle for the purposes of obtaining any evidence relating to that offence. – Holly?"

"Sarge."

"Can you tell me if you have a mobile phone in the car, Mr Booth, or any other sort of electronic device – laptop, PDA?"

"No. No, my phone's here – look, I—"

"Do you have any other phones at all – here or at home?"

"No."

"Sarge... Down by the seat."

"What about that phone? Is that yours?"

"No. I mean, yes, but it's an old one. I don't even know if it works. I'd forgotten it was there."

"Okay. Any others you might have forgotten about?"

"No – no. Honestly – listen – listen – does – does Lauren have to know? I mean… She doesn't have to come with us too, does she? Please? I really— I don't think I could face that."

"All right. It's probably better if she doesn't. I'll see if I can get someone to take her home."

"Thank you."

"Danny? Holly and I will take Mr Booth. Can you get a car for Lauren?"

"Sure."

"Okay, Mr Booth. This way."

"Dad? What's going on? Where are you going?"

"It's okay, sweetheart. Just stay with the officer – he'll get you home. I'll see you in a bit, okay?"

"But I don't understand."

"It's all right, sweetie. Just do as I said, okay? I love you."

"You know what I've got to do now, right?" Woods asked as he closed the door. In the back of the car Colin Booth sat with his head bowed.

"Call the DI?" Holly said.

Woods nodded. "She's going to love this. She banged on for half an hour last night about the TPO scheme being a political stunt, so this is going to go down like a cup of cold sick."

"Not poached salmon?"

Woods gave her a beady look. "Careful, Ms Blades, you'll cut yourself."

"Sorry, Sarge."

"Yeah, well... The risotto would have been better."

27.

CADOGAN ESTATE
16:35 HRS

The ambulance pulled away, its siren starting up as it did so, and Sam approached Oz, who was giving an update to Control.

"How bad is it?" Sam asked when Oz had signed off.

"Not life-threatening," Oz said. "We'll follow them down in a minute. Find the knife?"

Sam shook his head. "He could've taken it with him, the guy who did it. IC1, about eighteen, jeans and trainers, leather jacket, fair hair."

Oz looked to where Drew Alford and Skank were standing, both smoking as they watched the proceedings.

"Is that what they told you?"

"Yeah. Alford says he wasn't here when it happened. The other one – Winnard – says he saw it but he doesn't know who the attacker was."

"And if he did he wouldn't tell us. Whoever it was must've had some bottle though, fronting up to Tyler Smith."

He took a moment, thinking about it, then said, "Okay, put out an all-units on the description. I'll see if they know who called the ambulance, which they won't either."

28.

INCIDENT ROOM
MORNINGSTAR RD STATION
17:35 HRS

"Jesus Christ, Ray," DI Connors said. "It's bloody Sunday evening. And what's she doing here? I thought we talked about this last night."

"*You* talked about it," Ray Woods said, unfazed. "I just listened. Anyway, she's the one who nailed him."

Thank you!

At the other end of the room Holly sent out a silent blessing to the DS. She didn't look up from her typing though. She could sense that the DI was looking at her and knew the best thing was to pretend to be invisible.

"How?" Connors said in the end. "You're still talking about the same victim, right? So how the fuck do you get from an attempted rape with one suspect to grooming and underage sex with another? I mean, who is this guy Booth anyway?"

"Father of Ashleigh's best friend, Lauren Booth."

"And he's admitted it?"

"Not in so many words, but we've got texts between him and Ashleigh on a phone in his possession and his DNA's going to match the samples from Ashleigh's rape kit."

"You're sure about that?"

"Can't see it going any other way."

There was a pause then and Holly could sense the DI pacing irritably. Then she said: "Okay. Interview Booth and see what he's got to say for himself. Has he asked for a brief?"

"Not so far."

"And Ashleigh's still in the Vic?"

"Yeah."

"Okay, I'll take Wondergirl and talk to her."

"You don't want to interview Booth – let me go to the Vic?"

"No."

"Okay – Holly?"

"Sarge?" Holly stood up and moved round the desk as if she hadn't heard any of the previous conversation.

"We're going to the Vic," Connors told her. "Get your coat."

The DI didn't speak to Holly again until they were seated in her car and pulling out of the yard. Then she said: "My lecture about not running before you could walk didn't go in then."

"No, ma'am," Holly said. "I mean, yes it did but—"

"But you chose to ignore it."

"I just thought— I just thought there was something we'd missed, ma'am," Holly said. "And then the more I found out…"

"Right," Connors said dryly. "The hole just kept getting deeper."

She paused to look both ways at a junction, then pulled out and cancelled the indicator.

"So tell me," she said. "From the beginning. Tell me how you got to where you are: from Ashleigh to Alford to Booth."

29.

HUCKNALL WARD
QUEEN VICTORIA HOSPITAL
18:16 HRS

Ashleigh was half asleep in the dimly lit room when they arrived, but as the nurse showed them in she roused herself and sat up. She said yes when the nurse asked if she'd like a drink.

"Mum went home," Ashleigh told Connors. "There was no point in her staying."

"Would you like me to ask her to come back? I can if you'd prefer."

Holly thought that Ashleigh might well have preferred it, if only as a distraction, but in the end she shook her head. "No, it's okay," she said. "She could do with a break." She looked at Holly. "Has something happened?"

The DI took a seat on the edge of the bed, more friendly and approachable than Holly had seen her before.

"Ashleigh, I need you to tell us about Colin Booth – about your relationship with him."

"What?" Ashleigh said. "I don't know what you mean."

DI Connors held off for a moment, as if assessing the girl's expression, then she said: "I think you should know that Colin's been arrested."

"What? Why? – I don't know what— What's going on?"

Connors said nothing and Holly knew it was her cue.

"He's Bic, isn't he?" she said gently. "Colin."

Ashleigh shook her head. "I don't know anyone called Bic. I told you before."

"We've seen your phone," Holly said. "The texts between you and Bic. And we've got Colin's phone too. He was outside the hospital earlier and we talked to him."

"What– What do you mean? What did he say?"

"What do you think he might have said?" Connors asked.

"I don't know, do I? I don't know what all this is about." There was a note of rising distress in Ashleigh's voice. "Look– Look, I don't want to– I don't feel very well. Can't you just leave it? Come back tomorrow?"

"We can't do that," Connors said. "This is serious and you need to tell us the truth now – you were with Colin on Friday night, weren't you? After you left Lauren, before the accident. You went to meet him, didn't you?"

"No!"

"Ashleigh, we know you did," Holly said, as firm as she was gentle. "It's okay. You can tell us. You're not in any trouble, but we need to know."

She reached across the bed and took Ashleigh's hand. And as she did so Ashleigh's head slumped forward and her tears started to flow.

"He said... He said we – we had to stop," she sobbed. "He said he couldn't – we shouldn't see each other any more. He didn't want to meet me or for me to come to the house to see Lauren, or anything. He said it was getting too difficult, too dangerous. But I couldn't— I couldn't just stop like that… I love him. He's— He loves me too, I know he does. I know!"

Holly held Ashleigh's hand tighter. "How long have you been seeing him – meeting up with him?" she asked.

Ashleigh shook her head. "Only three months. It started a few weeks before Christmas."

"And you had sex with him?"

A nod, then: "Not at first. At first it was just – just coffee, going for walks, talking, you know?"

She looked up at Holly then, wet tracks of tears on her cheeks but a sudden determination in her eyes. "He didn't force me," she said. "It was never— He was the one who didn't want to – for ages. It was me. You can't blame him. It was me. I wanted to do it. I just...I just wanted to show how much I loved him."

"When was the last time you had sex with him?" Connors asked.

"Thursday. But he was...he wasn't the same. He said Anna, his wife, had been asking questions. He was worried."

"But you still went round to the house with Lauren on Friday," DI Connors said.

Ashleigh nodded. "I'd been texting him but he hadn't replied. I didn't know what was – what was going on." She looked at Holly to see if she understood.

Holly nodded. "So what happened on Friday?" she asked.

Ashleigh rubbed her eyes. "It was horrible. He said we had

to stop. It was too risky. And I— I said all sorts of things. I was a bitch."

"Did you have a row?"

Ashleigh nodded. "I tried to get him to change his mind. But he wouldn't. He just said – he said he loved me but we had to forget what had happened and try and start again without each other."

"So then what happened?"

"I shouted at him. I was crying. I don't know. I just couldn't stand it, so in the end I just went – ran off and left him." She paused, swallowed hard.

"It's okay," Holly said. "Just take your time."

Ashleigh sniffed. "I was just walking, crying. I don't know how long, but then I saw Drew and I thought – I thought, okay, if Colin thinks I've been seeing someone else that'll make him realise how much he wants me. So – so then I went up to Drew and said hello."

"Because you wanted Colin to feel jealous," Holly said.

Ashleigh picked at the sheet on the bed. "It wasn't— I didn't mean it for real," she said. "Not with Drew. I just thought if I snogged him or something… I knew he'd tell someone afterwards, then Lauren'd hear and if she told Colin… I thought, he'd have to call me then."

On the edge of the bed DI Connors drew a slow breath. "Can you tell us what happened then – with Drew?"

Ashleigh didn't meet her eye. She looked at the bed cover. "I told him I— I said, just snogging, and at first it was okay.

But then he— He was touching and...he wouldn't stop. He wouldn't— He wouldn't let go. He said he knew I wanted it, even when I pushed him off. I knew if he...if he could— So I pushed him again, really hard and then I just ran."

30.

INTERVIEW ROOM 3
MORNINGSTAR RD STATION
18:19 HRS

"How old is Ashleigh, do you know?"

"Yes."

"How old?"

"Fourteen."

"The same age as your daughter?" Woods said.

"Yes."

"Okay. So can you tell me the nature of your relationship with Ashleigh?"

For several seconds Booth said nothing, just stared at the table.

"Colin?"

Slowly Booth shook his head, still saying nothing.

"Was it a sexual relationship?" Woods asked.

Another moment of stillness, then finally Booth nodded.

"For the tape, please."

"Yes."

In the chair next to Woods, Danny Simmons shifted, but Woods remained still.

"Do you know that the age of sexual consent in this country is sixteen?"

"Yes."

"So you're admitting that you've had a sexual relationship with Ashleigh even though you knew she was under the age of consent – is that correct?"

Booth put his hand over his eyes, head bowed. "Yes."

"How many times have you had sex with her?" Danny Simmons said.

"I...I don't know."

"Two or three times? More than that?"

"More."

"Ten? Twenty?"

"No! Not as many as that."

"So somewhere between ten and twenty times."

"Yes." Booth's voice had a flat sound of defeat. "Yes, I suppose so."

"Do you know any other girls of about Ashleigh's age?"

"What?"

"Do you have a relationship with any other teenage girls?" Danny Simmons repeated clearly.

"What? No! No!" Booth had raised his head sharply at the question. "Look, it's not like that."

"Not like what?"

"Not like you're thinking. It isn't. There isn't anyone else. It's just Ashleigh. I...I didn't mean it to happen. It just did. But it's not– Not like you think."

"What is it like then?" Woods said.

"It's... Look, I knew we should stop, all right? I knew. I tried.

On Friday. I told her we couldn't do it any more. I knew the longer it went on... And with her coming to the house... I was afraid Lauren or Anna would realise, see something. I just couldn't do it any more."

"So what happened?" Woods asked.

"I went out. I told Anna I was going to the pub but I knew Ashleigh would know I was waiting for her. I sat in the car round the corner and when Ashleigh came a bit later I drove to the car park on Alma Way. That's where I told her."

He paused for a moment and drew a heavy breath, shook his head. "She...she got upset. Really upset. She was crying and saying she didn't want to stop and she knew I didn't want to either. She talked about running away – the two of us – and I told her there was no way we could do that. We just had to stop... In the end she just— She just got out of the car and ran."

"Did you go after her?"

Booth shook his head. "I thought— I thought it was better like that – if I didn't. I thought if I went after her she'd think I'd changed my mind, and I hadn't. I couldn't. So I just let her go."

He broke off then, finally looking directly at Woods. "I know it was— I know I shouldn't have... It just got out of hand. I've never done anything like that before, I swear it. Never."

For a moment Woods looked as if he might believe that. But then he reached below the desk and brought out a transparent evidence bag containing a mobile phone.

"For the benefit of the tape, I'm showing Mr Booth exhibit HB1. Is this your phone, Colin?"

Booth looked, then nodded. “Yes.”

“This is the phone you used to send and receive texts and calls with Ashleigh?”

“Yes.”

“Okay.”

Woods reached under the table again. This time he brought out a bag containing two more phones.

“What about these? Exhibit RW1 and RW2. Do you recognise them?”

Booth looked at the phones but said nothing.

“We found these in the boot of your car. What can you tell me about them?”

For a moment longer Booth remained still. Then he said: “I’d… I’d like to talk to a solicitor now. I don’t want to say any more.”

31.

QUEEN VICTORIA HOSPITAL
18:28 HRS

Holly pressed the call button by the lifts, listening as DI Connors spoke on the phone.

"Everything?" Connors asked. There was a pause, then she said: "Okay, we'll review when I get back. We're leaving the Vic now."

She rang off and turned to Holly. "Colin Booth's rolled over in interview. He's admitting an ongoing sexual relationship with Ashleigh."

"So we can charge him?"

Connors nodded. "For Ashleigh? Yes, for definite."

"What about the other phones, from the boot of his car? Has he said...?"

"No," Connors said. "He asked for a brief, so the interview's been suspended till he gets one."

"And Alford? I mean, if Ashleigh's willing to make a statement about the attempted rape..."

Connors looked at her speculatively. "One result's not enough for you?"

"Not if they've both committed offences," Holly said flatly.

"Yeah, well, it's Ashleigh's word against Alford's," Connors said. "And attempted rape's even harder to prove than rape itself."

"There's the forensic evidence to back it up though."

"Yeah, and if we take it to trial Alford's defence will use the fact that Ashleigh came on to him, and why. When a jury hears that it'll change the way they look at her. They're liable to think, *Oh, she's* that *kind of girl... Having it off with an older man, putting it about a bit...* It'll colour the way they think about her and give Alford the benefit of the doubt."

"That's wrong though, isn't it?" Holly said. "It doesn't matter *why* she was there – she said no. She didn't want to have sex with Alford and he knew that."

"I'm just telling you the way juries think," Connors said flatly.

The lift arrived and Connors waited until they'd got in before she spoke again. "Listen, we're going to send Booth down for what he did to Ashleigh, and if the other phones we found are linked to more girls, he's looking at ten years inside, maybe more. You should be happy with that."

"Yes...no, I am," Holly said.

Connors gave her a measured, impassive look, then seemed to relax – just a little. She said: "Yeah, well, if it was up to me I'd castrate them both with a pair of house bricks – Booth *and* Alford – but that would probably infringe their human rights. Pity though."

The lift came to a halt and when the doors opened they stepped out.

"I'll see what the CPS say about Alford," Connors said. "But don't get your hopes up. I'm pretty sure they'll let it go. Just be satisfied with Booth for the time being, okay? Take what you can get."

"Yes, ma'am."

"Good," Connors said.

32.

EMERGENCY DEPT
QUEEN VICTORIA HOSPITAL
18:35 HRS

"Do you know him?" Sam asked. "Had you seen him before?"

Tyler Smith shook his head. "I dunno who he was."

He was lying on a trolley in a cubicle with the curtains drawn. He wore a surgical gown and there was a drip going into his arm. He didn't look as pale as he had back at the precinct, Sam thought, but his face was still drawn and pained – nowhere near as tough or as menacing as he'd been when he'd split Charlie Atkins's lip yesterday.

"So why did he attack you?"

"I dunno."

Sam glanced to the foot of the bed where Oz was standing, listening and watching patiently. It had been his idea for Sam to do the questioning, but the lack of success didn't seem to worry him.

"It must've been about *something*," Sam insisted, turning back to Tyler. "Was there an argument?"

"No."

"So he just walked up to you and stabbed you – is that what you're saying?"

"Yeah."

Sam knew Tyler was lying but there didn't seem any way to break through the brick wall and he was becoming frustrated.

"Must be a change, you being the one on the receiving end. How's that feel?"

Tyler Smith gave him a dark look but said nothing.

"Listen," Sam said. "If it's some kind of grudge and you're afraid of him..."

"What?" For the first time Tyler Smith showed a reaction. "I ain't afraid of him, that little—" He stopped himself.

"So you do know who he is."

"No. No comment."

At last Oz seemed to have heard enough. He shifted and said, "Okay, Tyler, have it your own way. You can tell Drew you were a good boy and kept quiet. But if I hear of anything that sounds like tit-for-tat over this, I'm coming looking for you – right?"

Tyler had shifted uncomfortably at the mention of Drew Alford and for a second seemed about to reply, but then he looked away.

Outside the cubicle Sam put his pocketbook away. "That was crap," he said, dispirited.

Oz shrugged. "Not really."

"Maybe we should have given it a bit longer."

"Nah. He was never going to tell us who it was. Only thing you can do is warn him off from trying to even the score."

"Think it'll work?"

"Maybe – least until he's healed up. Then it'll depend on what Alford wants – whether he can keep a lid on it, whether he wants to. No telling there."

"So we just wait and see what happens."

"Yep." Oz looked at his watch. "Come on, we're supposed to be off."

33

It was dark and there were only the two of them. They stood near one of the wet benches in the precinct, both with their hoods up like cowls. Every so often Drew Alford's features were dimly lit as he drew on his cigarette. Ryan Atkins didn't smoke.

"If Tyler says it was Charlie, Charlie's going to say why. The car and the shop. Self-defence."

"That's not what Skank and Rizza'll say."

Ryan nodded. He'd expected something like that. "So?"

Alford sniffed, appearing to think about it. "You thought about what I said before?"

"Yeah."

"So...? – If you're in with us, that's it. Tyler's gonna keep quiet."

"And he stays away from Charlie."

"Course."

"He'd better."

"He will. He does what I tell him."

Ryan took a beat, then he said flatly: "Okay."

Alford nodded and flipped his cigarette away. He reached into the pocket of his hoodie and took out a wad of tissues wrapped round something harder. He held it out to Ryan.

"That's yours – or Charlie's. Thought you'd want it back. I'd dump it if it was me though."

Ryan took the bundle. He could feel the shape of the knife through the tissues without having to unwrap it. He also knew that by accepting it he was confirming the agreement to go in with Alford.

"Yeah," Ryan said. He put the bundle away. "I'll see you later then." He took a step to one side.

"You going home?" Alford asked, shifting.

"Yeah. Why?"

"I'll go with you. I want to check something out in your block."

"What?"

Alford shook his head. "Not yet. Later."

For a moment Ryan hesitated. Then he started out of the precinct with Alford beside him: two hooded figures, almost indistinguishable from each other.

34.

CUSTODY SUITE
MORNINGSTAR RD STATION
19:17 HRS

Behind the custody desk Sergeant Stafford read from the form in his hand. In front of him Colin Booth stood with his head bowed and his solicitor beside him.

"Colin Ian Booth, you are charged that on February 3rd this year at Sandmile Lane you did engage in sexual activity with Ashleigh Jane Jarvis, namely full sexual intercourse, contrary to Section 9 of the Sexual Offences Act 2003. I have considered bail in this case and have decided that it will not be granted because other offences of a similar nature are still being investigated against you. You will appear before Weston Magistrates Court tomorrow morning at 10 a.m. Do you have anything you wish to say?"

Colin Booth shook his head.

"Seen enough?" Woods asked. They were some distance away: the DS, Danny Simmons and Holly.

She nodded. "Thanks, Sarge."

They turned away from the charge desk and headed for the doors into the rest of the nick. Somewhere out of sight there was the sound of a rowdy drunk protesting his innocence.

"So is that it then?" Holly asked. "I mean, do I need to do anything else?"

"No. Go home," Woods said. "You're off tomorrow, right?"

"Till Wednesday."

"Good. Stick your head into CID then – I'll tell you if we need anything else on your statements."

"Course, by rights you should be buying drinks now," Danny said. "First time you bang someone up on a charge carrying more than a year inside you buy a round for everyone involved."

"Pity I can't then," Holly said. "Least, not legally."

"No. And you'd never try and pass for older than you are, right?" Woods said.

"Me? Never," Holly told him. "So does that mean you're not pretending I'm twenty-six any more?"

Woods glanced back at Booth, then pushed the door open. "Yeah, I reckon we'll drop that now," he said.

Holly saw his sober expression and nodded. "Okay," she said.

They moved into the corridor and Woods paused when they reached the turning to CID.

"You got a good one," he told Holly. "It didn't go unnoticed, okay?"

And with that, he was moving on.

Danny Simmons stayed a moment longer. "He means it," he said. "Just so you know."

Holly nodded. "Thanks."

For a second she was about to say something else, but then had the sense not to. Danny gave her a smile and headed off after Woods.

35

Ryan sat on the bed next to Charlie. The sound of the TV in the sitting room was audible through the wall.

"They'll leave you alone, but stay out of their way, okay?"

"What did you do?" Charlie said, even though he was afraid of what the answer would be.

Ryan shook his head. "Nothing," he said. Then he saw Charlie's expression. "Listen, don't worry about it, okay? Nothing's going to happen. I saw Drew. I sorted it."

"You sure?" Charlie's face made it clear how much he wanted to believe it was true.

"Sure," Ryan said. "It's all over. Forget it, okay?"

Charlie hesitated, then finally nodded. "Thanks, Ry," he said.

"Nah," Ryan said, then he rubbed Charlie's head and gave him an easy-going shove as he stood up to leave the room.

And because he had turned away, Charlie couldn't see that Ryan's expression didn't match the lightness and certainty of his words. It couldn't – not now that he'd agreed to let Drew Alford come and go as he liked in Cloudsley House – and not now that he was tied in with the Kaddy Boys and whatever they did.

36.

FEMALE LOCKER ROOM
MORNINGSTAR RD STATION
19:32 HRS

Shift change had been and gone and in the locker room Holly was alone. There was only a faint hint of condensation and deodorant left in the air.

She knew she should be pleased – celebrating even – because Colin Booth was going to go down. But the satisfaction was tempered by knowing what the effects were going to be – on Lauren Booth, her mother, and on Ashleigh Jarvis. Somehow it didn't seem right to be pleased by the fact that all their lives had just been blown apart.

Back in the corridor Holly fastened her coat as she headed for the station's exit.

"Hol! Hang on."

Holly looked back, then stopped.

"I thought you'd be off by now," she said when Sam caught up with her. He was in civvies as well.

"I've been down at the hospital with Oz. One of the Kaddy Boys was stabbed."

"Drew Alford?"

Sam shook his head. "Tyler Smith."

"Pity," Holly said, and Sam could tell that she meant it.

He pushed the door open and they stepped outside. The wind had dropped and left a clear, cold night with a promise of frost.

"You got that guy Booth for underage sex though – right?"

"Yeah."

"So? Come on," Sam said, cajoling. "First major arrest. Bloody hell. If it was me… Hey, I did hack the phone though."

"Yeah, yeah, you were a vital part of the investigation," Holly said, finally lightening up.

"'Vital'? Excellent!"

Holly laughed. "I suppose it wasn't bad for a Sunday," she said.

LATER

On Monday 7th February the Crown Prosecution Service reviewed the case against Drew Alford for the attempted rape of Ashleigh Jarvis. It decided there was insufficient evidence to bring a charge with a realistic prospect of conviction. Drew Alford was not arrested or interviewed again about the incident.

On June 9th at Weston Crown Court, Colin Booth pleaded guilty to three counts of sexual activity with a child. Six other counts were taken into consideration. He also pleaded guilty to two separate counts of grooming a young person for the purposes of sexual activity. He was sentenced to a total of twelve years' imprisonment and told that on release he would be required to sign the Sex Offenders Register indefinitely.

Anna and Lauren Booth left Weston a month after Colin Booth was arrested. Anna Booth was granted a divorce from her husband on the grounds of unreasonable behaviour. She and Lauren now live in the Midlands.

Ashleigh Jarvis made a full recovery from her head injury. She and her mother still live at the same address but Ashleigh now attends a different school.

Tyler Smith also made a full recovery and continues to live on the Cadogan Estate.

Acknowledgements

I have been writing about the police and criminals for quite a while and over that time I've been helped by numerous people – including many serving and retired police officers. They have all been exceptionally generous with their time and expertise, but I must give a special mention to Clive Blake, Keith Gausden, Malcolm Haddow, Trevor Hermes and Jackie Malton – most of what I know about coppers is down to them.

For this book I owe particular thanks to Dr Iain Beardsell for medical guidance, and to Keith Gausden for police advice. The credit for accuracy is theirs, the responsibility for errors and dramatic licence is mine.

I would also like to thank Jasmin Kilby for reading the early draft; my agent, Stephanie Thwaites, for her exceptional patience and faith, and – of course – the wonderful team at Usborne Publishing.

Chris Ould

"To paraphrase Raymond Chandler,
I try to write stories about people who
commit realistic crime for real reasons and
with real consequences – not just to provide
a convenient excuse for the cops to
turn up and solve it."

introducing

Chris Ould

the freshest blood in YA crime fiction

Hear from Chris Ould on writing crime fiction

What do you think is the key to writing authentic crime fiction?

Research. If my books seem authentic it's because I try to create stories that the reader could imagine happening to them, or to people they know. Talking to real coppers, reading about and researching real crimes and then imagining the circumstances that could have made the crime happen are what make the stories seem real – at least, I hope they do.

How do you keep the pace of the books fast-moving and gripping?

It's all to do with combining the characters with the plot. If the reader cares about characters like Holly and Sam and then I put them in situations where they may be in danger or have to take a risk, then the reader wants to know what happens next. There always has to be jeopardy of some kind and the TPOs need to work hard to find out the truth. If the answers come too easily or the reader can predict the next move then I haven't done my job properly.

Do you have any rules for your writing?

Just two: Write at least a thousand words every day and don't cheat the reader. By that I mean, don't rely on coincidence to make something happen, and if the plot requires a character to act in a certain way it must be a credible thing for them to do. I also try to stick as closely as possible to real police procedure, although occasionally you do have to use a bit of dramatic licence to keep the story moving. No one wants to read about the endless form-filling which is part of a real copper's everyday work.

Why do you think crime fiction is so enduringly popular?

I think it's partly because crime fiction is infinitely renewable – give three different writers the same basic crime and they will all tackle it differently. Their characters will react differently and they will each have different motivations.

As well as that, though, we're all touched by crime, directly or indirectly – maybe it's just seeing reports on the TV, or knowing someone who's been mugged or burgled. The trouble is, we rarely get to see the whole picture: once the police leave the scene we don't know what they do next or how they do it, so crime novels can give us an insight into what's normally hidden. I think we all like the idea that we've managed to sneak a look behind the scenes.

You've written extensively for television. Does that influence the way you write the *Street Duty* novels and what are the differences between the two forms of writing?
I'm sure *Street Duty*'s style is quite heavily influenced by my screenwriting, particularly the pace and the dialogue. Most of the chapters in the book are individual scenes and I did that on purpose. I wanted the book to unfold like a movie or TV drama, so the reader had almost the same experience as they would watching it on screen. The biggest difference between writing scripts and novels is that when you're writing a novel, you have the chance to be more subtle, especially with characterisation. You can go deeper into what a character is thinking and feeling and explore why they do what they do.

Which do you prefer; writing scripts or novels?
Definitely novels. With most TV series you have to write to a brief or storyline supplied by the programme and you only have a limited number of options. With a novel you're much more your own boss: you have to come up with the characters, the plot, the whole thing. Sometimes that makes it harder to get right, but if it's not working you can change it without asking someone else's permission!

As teenagers, how to do you feel the characters of Holly and Sam differ from fictional adult detectives?
The majority of adult detectives in fiction seem to be battered, cynical, world-weary, divorced, alcoholic and bitter, and that's just the upbeat ones! The great difference between these older characters and Holly and Sam is that the TPOs are exactly the opposite. As teenagers they haven't yet seen enough to have had the enthusiasm knocked out of them. They're still willing to take people at face value (even if they later find out they shouldn't have) and above all they want to be coppers more than anything else in the world. Naturally they have doubts and problems like all teenagers, but their optimism and enthusiasm for the job – whatever it throws their way – is what I love about them.

You portray the Cadogan Estate so vividly in the book, it's like another character. Is it based on a particular place?
The Cadogan Estate is an amalgam of different places, impressions and locations I've come across over the years. I tried to capture elements that were common to a lot of real places. I lived in a pretty rough part of London's East End for several years and although *Street Duty* isn't set in London, a lot of the Cadogan Estate probably comes from that.

And finally, what's next for Holly, Sam, Ryan and Drew?
To answer that would spoil the surprise! The next book moves them all forward in different ways and Holly in

particular has some hard choices to make. Longer term, I think it would be interesting to follow the TPOs through to becoming fully qualified police officers, but that's a long way in the future. There's a lot that can happen to them before they get there.

STREET DUTY: CASE TWO

GEMMA loves DEAN, but he's making her do things that she doesn't want to do.

RYAN did a deal to join up with the KADDY BOYS, but now he's in, there's no getting out.

TAZ is being paid to be an informant for the COPS, but is she getting too close to the TARGETS?

And when HOLLY attends her first suspicious DEATH, is she ready for the impact that being a COPPER can have on your family, your friends and your LIFE?

Especially when you KNOW one of the suspects...

REAL LIFE, REAL CRIME AND REAL DRAMA COLLIDE IN THE SECOND, COMPULSIVE INSTALMENT OF STREET DUTY

ISBN: 9781409549499

EPUB: 9781409557333 MOBI: 9781409557340

COMING IN 2013

www.streetdutycasenotes.com

for exclusive **STREET DUTY** content